DANGER ZONE

DAVID KLASS

SCHOLASTIC INC.
New York Toronto London Auckland Sydney

No part of this publication may be reproduced in whole or in part, or stored in a retrieval system, or transmitted in any form or by any means, electronic, mechanical, photocopying, recording, or otherwise, without written permission of the publisher. For information regarding permission, write to Scholastic Inc., 555 Broadway, New York, NY 10012.

ISBN 0-590-48591-1

24 23 22 21 20 19 18 17 16   6 7 8/0

Printed in the U.S.A.   01

For Gaopalelwe Mokwena
and Misha McK

CHAPTER ONE

I don't know if you've ever been in a zone.

There's nothing else like it in sports. There's probably nothing else like it in life. Who knows why you slip into one? Or why you suddenly fall out of it? But when and if you ever do find the magical doorway, watch out, because for a few minutes you'll be capable of just about anything.

The Granham High School gymnasium sits behind the school in a grassy field at the southeast corner of town. We rarely get to see the grass — for seven months a year Minnesota is covered by snow. The population of Granham is a little over eight thousand, and it looked as if half the town was packed into the rows of bleachers on either side of the court that night in early March when I went into a zone.

I had started slowly, and so had our team. "Doyle, Doyle, Doyle," the fans roared expectantly. Not Granham, but Doyle. James Giacomo Doyle. Trust an Irish father and an Italian mother to come up with a smorgasbord of a name. My friends call me Jim. My fans call me Doyle. In all modesty, the assembled townspeople were shouting out my name, rather than the name of

1

the school, because I sort of *was* the team. When I was hot, Granham won. When I was mediocre, we still usually won. When I was lousy, which didn't happen too often, we always lost.

On this night, so far, I was barely mediocre. It was our final regular season game of the year, against Eisenhower High, and they were playing me real tough. They had a lightning-fast guard named Rushman who was marking me man to man, sticking to me like he was glued to my chest. He had two inches on me, and remarkably fast feet. Every time I touched the ball he got help from one of his teammates. When I went up for a jumpshot I always had two or three hands in my face. When I tried to penetrate inside, their big men rotated over to help close off the lanes.

"Doyle, Doyle, Doyle." It's strange to hear two thousand people chanting your name like a cavalry charge, and not to be able to do anything.

Time after time when I was double- and triple-teamed I fed the ball to an open teammate, but for the most part they missed wide-open shots. They were a good bunch of guys, the other Granham players, but none of them could really put the ball in the hoop with any consistency. In fact, some of them were downright rotten. At the quarter we were trailing by five points. As we walked off after the half, we were down by twelve.

I only had nine points, which was a dismal half for me.

Janey, my girlfriend, watched sympathetically as I filed off the hardwood floor toward the passageway beneath the dark iron supports for the old bleachers. She's a cheerleader and she can yell with the best of them, but she's very sensitive and can tell when I don't feel like hearing too much loud encouragement. "You'll turn it around," she whispered as we walked past.

"Sure. Thanks. Good luck with the halftime show." I managed a smile, and then I headed for our locker room.

The silence of the locker room is a welcome break when you're losing and not playing particularly well. Coach Brauner gave his usual pep talk. Diagrams were drawn on a small blackboard. We were reminded that our game was being televised throughout the county by a local TV station. Have pride, he said. Tighten up on D, he said. Get the ball to Doyle and run screens for him, he said.

I sat alone for a minute, after the pep talk. Nine points. A lousy half. Coach Brauner came over and sat down next to me. He had been a star player himself, both at the high school and college level, and he knew what I was thinking and feeling. "Just keep shooting and it'll come," he said.

"Let's hope so."

"It will. Listen, some men are here who want to talk to you after the game."

"Scouts?" I had gotten used to college scouts, even though I'm just a junior. I guess I'd already talked to scouts from most of the basketball powerhouse colleges in America.

"No," he said. "Not from a college, anyway."

I looked at him. "What did they come for?"

"I don't know. Something about an international competition this coming summer. But they can tell you. I just didn't want you and Janey to wander off before they got a chance to say their piece. Because I know they came a long way to see you, and they're flying out later tonight."

"Okay," I said. "If they even want to talk to me after seeing this game."

He slapped me on the back. "Keep shooting. You'll heat up."

"Can't get much colder."

He walked away, and I tried to get my concentration together for the second half. I closed my eyes and re-laxed my whole body, breathing evenly. In the back of my mind, the thought that two scouts from some sort of international competition had flown to Minnesota and then driven all the way to Granham to see me play was kicking around. I sure hadn't shown them much. With an effort, I drove all such thoughts out of my mind and forced myself to concentrate on the second half.

"Doyle, Doyle, Doyle." Our bleachers erupted into cheers when we walked back onto the court.

I glanced up at the scoreboard. Twelve points behind. A long way to come back. Next I looked over at the cheerleaders, and Janey caught my eyes and gave me a smile to start the third quarter off with. She has long black hair and hazel-brown eyes, and I can't imagine anyone ever looking prettier than she does in her cheer-leader uniform.

It's an old gym — it was built just after the Second World War. The bleachers are the same color wood as the hardwood floor, and for some reason it always reminds me of a big cigar box. It even has a sweet, almost tobaccolike, smell. Lights are suspended from a spiderweb of iron bars just beneath the ceiling. A big American flag dangles down from the center of that network of iron. On either side of the flag hang two league championship banners from a decade or so past, when Granham was a regional powerhouse.

The second half started out exactly the way the first one ended. We missed a jumpshot. They rebounded, got a fast break, and scored at their end. Fourteen points behind. Almost beyond reach — especially the way we were playing.

I took the ball upcourt and dished a nice bounce pass to Charley Connors, one of our gawky forwards. He had a wide-open shot, but instead of taking it he passed the ball back to me. Rushman was right in my face, and their other guard came over to help out. I feinted right, then left, got a tiny bit of daylight, and threw up what would have been an NBA three-pointer. I knew it was in as it came off my fingers. Nothing but net.

Rushman dribbled the ball up for them. He stopped at midcourt and looked left for a second, contemplating a pass. I darted in and slapped the ball away, and then recovered it and flew downcourt for a layup. He was quick and somehow he got back, but I gave him two head-fakes, the second of which nearly pulled him up out of his jockstrap. Then, when he was in the air, I swung around him and laid it in with a picture-perfect reverse layup.

"Doyle, Doyle, Doyle."

As I bounced the ball up on our next possession, I was beginning to feel it. I faked a pass, dribbled to the top of the key, and put up a fadeaway jumper with two hands waving in my face. Swish. Nothing but net.

We got another turnover. I found Aldrich, our center, inside. He shot from less than three feet but he has stone hands and I sensed he was going to miss. I started running just as he shot, left the ground as the ball cleared the far side of the hoop, and was soaring up there all alone to tap it home. It felt as if I could have jumped right over the backboard if I had wanted to.

"Doyle, Doyle, Doyle."

Their coach called a time-out. "Hey, that was great . . ." Aldrich started to say to me, but Coach Brauner tapped him on the shoulder.

"Don't say anything to him," Brauner told him. "Just leave him alone."

I sat there, feeling the tips of my fingers, my heart keeping rhythm with the chanting of the crowd, awash in a secret spotlight that magically followed me step for step, shot for shot, second by second.

"You don't wanna snap him out of it. He's in a zone." I heard Coach Brauner's voice, but the spoken words sounded strange — musical and somehow distant. Everything was poetry. Zone, zone, zone. Hold the phone. Leave him alone. Where the buffalo roam. I'm in a zone. Zone, zone, zone.

We were playing again. I found myself triple-teamed. Put it up anyway from twenty feet out. Swish. Nothing but net.

Their faces as they looked at me. Their eyes . . . they were beginning to look like the victims in a horror film. Some of them were shaking their heads. Some appeared to be afraid. Rushman looked as if he wanted to break both my knees.

Next possession. I took it inside, a quick crossover step, put it up lefty off the backboard. Bingo.

Zone, zone, zone. The basket's a big orange ice cream cone. Slam, jam, wham it home. I'm in a zone.

Rushman tried a layup of his own. I picked his pocket and started downcourt with the ball. Somehow the other four guys on their team raced back. All of them were ready for me. Four on one. I took it into the right corner. Near our bench. In front of our fans. "Doyle, Doyle." In front of Janey. Their four guys swarmed me. I saw them coming, like they were moving in slow motion. A wall of arms and hands. I picked up my dribble, elevated twenty-five inches above the hardwood, got a split-second look at the rim above their fingertips as they went up also, and let the ball go. Swish. Nothing but net.

We won by fifteen points. I finished with forty-three. There was a little mob scene. Players. Cheerleaders. Fans. A kiss from Janey. I kind of wished my mom could have been there, but of course she was working.

Rushman came over. "I've never seen anything like

that," he said, shaking my hand. "I couldn't do nothing with you. Nothing."

"I just got hot," I told him. "You played good."

Their coach shook my hand. Then he made his whole team shake my hand. It was kind of embarrassing, but I did my best to carry it off. It's not like I'm anything special in any other way but basketball. B student. Can't dance. Can't sing. Not bad-looking but no Brad Pitt. I try to be nice and polite, but I do have a temper. Try to help out my mom, but I probably don't do enough at home or at the store. Anyway, I'm not exactly the president or the Pope, and it felt strange to be shaking all their hands. But I guess I understood it. When you come out of a zone, people sense that you've been to a place they'll never visit, and they want to touch you and feel some of the magic.

I showered. Changed into jeans, a flannel shirt, a wool sweater. Did a quick interview outside the locker room for our local paper. And then I followed Brauner into the coaches' room, where two men in dark suits were waiting for me.

One of the men was black, one white. Both were well over six feet tall. They were in their late thirties or forties and they both looked as if they had scored a lot of baskets themselves in the not-too-distant past.

Coach Brauner said, "No one will disturb you here. Talk as long as you want." And then he left and shut the door behind him, leaving the three of us alone.

There was a momentary silence. The black man stepped forward first, held out his right hand, and gave me a big smile. He had a neatly trimmed pencil-thin mustache. "Let me see the hand that scored all those baskets." His hand was enormous — my palm seemed almost to disappear into his grip. He didn't let go right away, but kept shaking and smiling at me. "I'm Terry Griffin. This is Chris McNeil."

I shook hands with Chris next. "Jim, we almost left after the half," Chris said, making a smiling confession. "Boy, are we glad we stayed. I haven't seen a display of long-range shooting like that in a long time."

"You pumped us both up," Terry agreed. "Just watching made me want to get on the floor and show Chris here a few of the old moves."

"The first half I was terrible," I said.

"I can't even remember the first half," Chris replied. "All I remember is these outrageous three-point shots coming from every direction, and I said to Terry, 'We've found our shooting guard.' Watch out, Spain. Watch out, Italy. Cuba, beware!"

Terry glanced at his watch. "Unfortunately, we have to leave almost right away for Los Angeles. So we'd better get to the point. You know about the Olympics. Then there's the national college team. And the Mc-Donald's All-American High School Tournament. The international interest in youth basketball is such that the age brackets are being moved down all the time. This coming summer there's going to be the first ever world tournament for players seventeen and under."

I looked from one of them to the other, nodded, and shivered with nervous anticipation.

"It will be in June," Chris said. "One week to prepare, in Los Angeles. And then we fly over and play for three weeks — if we keep winning — in a tournament in Rome. Thirty-two countries are entered. Single elimination. It should really be something."

I stayed silent. The whole month of June. The thrill of what was about to be offered and the pain of what I was going to have to say were tying my tongue in double knots. A month. Far too long. Maybe it was for the best, anyway. . . .

"The tournament rules say we can only bring ten players over," Terry said. "You've had a lot less exposure than other kids in the big cities. And, to be frank, you've played against a lower level of opposition. But after what we saw today . . . we'd like to offer you a spot. One of ten. Out of every player your age in the entire country. Whatta ya say, Jimmy? Wanna come play for us, and represent the United States of America?"

"No," I whispered. And then, as they stared at me, "I can't. But thank you for the honor."

"Why not?" Terry wanted to know.

I shrugged. "Family reason."

"They don't like you to go so far away from home? We deal with those concerns a lot on the junior level. We'll call your father up and convince him."

"It's just my mom at home and . . . my two little sisters. There's really no way I could do it. But thanks again."

They looked at each other. Terry examined my face

for several seconds and then asked: "Jim, do you understand what we're offering you?"

I nodded.

"We know you never play in any of the regional camps and summer leagues for all-stars, even though you must get invited. Is it your game? Are you worried about how you'd stack up?"

"No, sir. Like I said, it's a family thing."

"The kind of family thing you don't want to talk about?"

"Thank you again for the honor. I know our team . . ." My voice broke and it took me several seconds to get control back. "I know the United States team will do real well." I could feel myself starting to lose it then, so I said a quick good-bye to both of them and hurried out of the room.

The last thing I saw as I hurried away was the two scouts for the national seventeen-and-under team coming out of the coaches' room. Terry looked after me with curiosity as Chris began to ask Coach Brauner a question.

"We know you never play in any of the regional

CHAPTER TWO

If the truth be known, I did a lot of my growing up in
a hardware store.

It's not very big — two twenty-foot-long aisles jam-
packed on both sides with hammers, saws, pliers,
wrenches, screwdrivers, locks, adhesives, cleaning supplies, and just about anything else anyone might need
around the house or yard.

My father bought and opened the store the year he
married my mother. He ran it by himself, at a slight
loss, till he collapsed behind the cash register and died
of a heart attack when I was eleven years old. Mom was
home that day, taking care of my two little sisters. I was
alone with Dad in the store, helping him shut up for the
night. I heard him gasp and fall, I called the police with
fingers shaking so badly that I could barely dial, and
then I rode with him to the hospital, holding his left
hand and willing him to keep breathing while the siren
shrieked overhead.

The last thing he said to me was the word *love*. Just
that one word, in a hoarse whisper. Love. He was trying
to tell me that he loved us. He left his widow and three
young children twenty thousand dollars in debt, with no

assets but a partially paid mortgage on a hardware store and the stock we had on our shelves.

People offered to take the store off our hands. Buy out our mortgage. Wipe away the debts. We'd be free and clear. Mom could go on welfare. Stay home and raise her kids. A few family friends even offered to give us some money.

My mother is a small woman with light brown hair and a soft voice that makes her seem almost fragile. When you first see her it's almost as if she's made of glass, and you worry that too loud a sound or too strong an action might shatter her. But she's probably the toughest person I've ever known in my life. When Dad died she took over his store, turned it into a money-maker, and paid off the mortgage year by year. She's never taken a dime from the government, except for Dad's veteran's insurance, which she said he earned for all of us.

She keeps the store open every day of the year except Christmas, New Year's, and July Fourth, from nine in the morning till seven at night. When she gets home around seven-thirty and picks up my two little sisters from our next-door neighbor, Mrs. Mills, Mom's face is tight with strain and her eyes are blurry with fatigue. As soon as she gets in the door she puts a kettle on to boil and then wets a towel with ice water and buries her face in it. She makes a cup of tea, puts on classical music — usually a piano concerto — and relaxes for fifteen minutes in a rocking chair.

She rocks back and forth, sipping the tea. No one is

allowed to talk to her during those fifteen minutes on penalty of death.

When her break is over she comes to life again, makes dinner, checks to make sure my sisters and I are finishing our homework, and does whatever else has to be taken care of around the house. I do what I can to help her, but I always feel I should find ways to do a lot more. And when I go out on weeknights, to celebrate basketball victories, I always feel a little bit guilty.

After the Eisenhower game I went out for hot chocolate at the Main Street Diner with Janey. She wanted to know about the mysterious men who had come to talk to me. I told her they were scouts and then changed the subject.

Janey and I are from different worlds. If I grew up in a hardware store, helping my father and then my mother during weekends and vacations, she grew up in a country club. Both her parents are doctors. Her father is a heart surgeon at the County Hospital in Chisholm. Her mother has her own general practice in town. Their house is in the best possible spot on Lakeview Road. It's a white colonial with six bedrooms, and I think you could fit my family's entire apartment in their high-ceilinged living room that looks out at Blackfoot Lake.

Janey's real smart, like her parents, and I could never figure out why she was wasting her time with an average guy like me. I guess maybe she had a weakness for the dramatics of hoopdom and the heroics of hardwood. That night in the Main Street Diner, as one person after another came over to our table to shake my hand or clap me on the back and say, "Great game," her pretty hazel eyes were glowing.

I was facing out the window of the diner, watching snowflakes sift down over the bare street and the two-foot-high mounds of snow and ice that had been pushed up onto the curbs by bulldozers earlier in the week. Elvis was crooning from the jukebox, there was the smell and sizzle of burgers, and Janey and I were holding hands under the Formica table. Everything was terrific except that I couldn't get the thought of an international basketball competition, in Europe, out of my mind.

"Are you okay?" Janey asked. "You looked sad for a minute."

"I was just remembering all those missed shots in the first half."

"I knew you would come back strong," she said. "You had that look in your eyes when you came back from the locker room after halftime."

"What look is that look?"

She scrunched up her face in an imitation of me trying to concentrate, and we both laughed. "What does it feel like to play that well?" she asked. "Do you know that your shots are all going to fall in?"

"When you're in a zone, you stop worrying about things like that. You just fall into the rhythm of the game and have fun."

"Well, it's amazing to watch," she said. "Do you want to have dinner here?"

This is one of our problems as a couple. Janey has

lots of spending money and free time, and she's always suggesting things I can't do. "Sorry. I have to head home."

"It's okay," she said.

"I'll walk you home."

"You don't have to."

"Are you going to stay here?"

"No."

"Then I want to walk you home."

"I'm not going to get buried in a snowdrift if I walk home alone," she said.

"I'm not worried about that," I told her. "I'm worried that you might run away with a tribe of Gypsy fortune-tellers."

She rolled her eyes, and we got up and put our coats on. The joke about the Gypsies is a running gag with us, because Janey is convinced that she has the power to tell the future. In every other way, she's the smartest and most rational girl I've ever met. But I can't shake her off this fortune-telling business, even though I don't believe it for a minute. So I tease her about it. At first it was astrology. Then she began reading palms. And while I try to joke about it, I don't understand how the child of two doctors can really think she has some sort of magical power.

We left the diner and the numbing wind blew snow against the bare skin of our faces. "Feels like spring is in the air," I muttered, shivering.

"Do you think it's really starting to get warmer?"

"I bet flowers are budding beneath the ice."

She giggled. "They say more snow tomorrow."

"Thanks. Could we have some hail and sleet, too?"

"Don't talk like a wimp."

"You call a guy who scored forty-three points a wimp?"

"There are high-scoring wimps and low-scoring wimps. It's not that cold out."

I put my arm around her, pulled her close, and kissed her. "Does that feel like being kissed by a wimp?"

"I'm not sure," she whispered. "Let me see again." And she kissed me back.

The snow had stopped falling when we reached her house. The lights were on downstairs, and I could see through the picture window that a big log fire was roaring away in the fireplace. "Do you want to come in for a minute?" she asked.

"I really better get home."

"'Bye."

We kissed again.

"I want to tell you a secret," Janey said. I bent my head and she whispered in my ear: "You were terrific tonight, but you're still a wimp."

"Why?"

"'Cause you won't tell me why you looked so sad in the diner. I never believed for one minute it had anything to do with you missing so many shots in the first half." Then she turned and hurried toward the house.

Like I said, she's much too smart for me.

I jogged home through the new-fallen powder, leaning forward into the cold night wind. I like Minnesota, but sometimes I fantasize about moving to Hawaii. Beach luaus, volcanos, hula girls on surfboards, sunny days in February and March . . .

My mom must have gotten home just a few minutes before me, because when I walked in she was in her chair, eyes closed, rocking back and forth to a piano concerto. I listened for a second. It was Beethoven's "Apassionata" — when you hear piano concertos nearly every night, you start to be able to identify the biggies.

Carrie and Ruthie, ages seven and eight, were doing their homework on the kitchen table. "Hi, Monsters," I said as I went past toward the refrigerator.

"Hi, Wheelhead," Carrie replied without looking up. For some reason she thinks my head looks like a wheel.

"You're late, Bug Eyes," Ruthie said. It's nice to have two such sweet little sisters.

"I had a game."

"So you had a stupid game. Did you win?"

"Of course."

"Were you a star?"

"A supernova."

"What's that?"

"A star that explodes and becomes brighter than anything else in the sky."

"How was Janey?" Ruthie asked with a giggle.

"Did you kiss her good-night?" Carrie wanted to know.

They're at that age when they love to tease me about my girlfriend. "Janey's fine, thank you." I carried the glass of juice into my room and closed the door. My bedroom just might be the smallest bedroom in the history of the world. The bed takes up about three quarters of the space. A dresser and a small desk fill up the rest. I can only pull the chair for the desk back about ten inches before it hits the footboard of the bed. When I get up at night to go to the bathroom and am too lazy to switch on the light, I always trip or knock my knee against something.

But I guess I shouldn't complain. Having my own room is a luxury. My mom, Ruthie, and Carrie all sleep in the same room, where my parents slept when my dad was alive.

I did a little bit of math homework, and then I had to stop because my stomach was growling, and it's a well-known scientific fact that it's impossible to do algebra problem sets when you can hear dinner cooking away and smell the smells and your stomach begins saying, "Go check it out. See what's on the stove. Go, go, go." So finally I closed my algebra book and went to see.

Mom had gotten out of her rocker and was cooking away. "Smells good," I said, hiding a question behind a compliment.

Lately we've had some friction around dinnertime, because my mom has been turning into more and more of a vegetarian. At first she decided that we shouldn't eat red meat. No beef. No lamb. No pork. That made some sense two ways — red meat's supposed to be bad for your heart, and it's also expensive. The only problem is that I kind of like a good steak or hamburger now and then.

From red meat, she moved on down the food chain. Rarely do I see turkey anymore. Or even chicken. Instead, she stays with fish, and lately the Doyle dinner table has seen a suspicious number of totally meatless, chickenless, and fishless dinners. We get pastas. Stuffed tomatoes. Eggplant steaks. Vegetable curries. I try not to complain too much, because I realize how hard she works and that we should be grateful for whatever we find on our table, but I have to confess that after a hard day of school and basketball practice, a meatless dinner just doesn't cut it.

"Orecchiette," she said. "It's a kind of ear-shaped pasta that in fact means 'ear' in Italian."

"Great. With what kind of sauce?"

"Good sauce," she said. "Set the table and help your little sisters finish their homework."

Setting the table sounded like more fun, so I did that first. Then I went to deal with the monsters. Luckily, they had both just finished their homework, so we sat on the couch, watched TV, and traded abuse till dinner was ready.

Ruthie brought in a salad. Carrie had the vegetable — broccoli. I carried in the pasta. Mom brought in the sauce in a covered red pot, and sat it down on a trivet. When she set it down I sniffed a few times, but I couldn't identify the smell. She looked at me and shook her head. "*Orecchiette con funghi e piselli.*"

"What does that mean in English?"

"With mushrooms and peas."

"Oh," I said. "Good." I stared down at my plate.

"It is good for you. And you should be grateful for it."

"Who says I'm not?"

"You look like somebody just rubbed sand on your tongue," Ruthie said.

I kicked her under the table and she kicked me back as we all joined hands and bowed our heads. My mom said a little prayer thanking God for giving us our dinner.

Then we dug in. Healthy food is better than no food, although I couldn't help dreaming about chunks of beef and pieces of chicken floating in the sauce. But there were just piddly peas and musty old mushrooms.

"How was your game tonight?" Mom asked.

"I got hot. I think there'll be a picture of me in the paper again." I thought about it, and decided not to mention the two scouts for the seventeen-and-under team. What was the point? "How're things at the store?" I asked instead.

"Slow," Mom said. "But they'll pick up. Gene Walters stopped in to chat. Soon as it gets warm, he's going to redo his whole back porch. He's so wonderful with his hands . . . does all the work himself."

Our hardware business is definitely seasonal. Our best two seasons are spring and fall; people buy tools and supplies to begin fixing things up after the long winter, and they stock up again to do last-minute repairs before the winter hits.

Early summer. One of our busiest times. When I was definitely needed to help out. A month-long tournament, starting at the end of May. In Europe. No way. Best not to even mention it.

After dinner, I did the dishes while Carrie dried and Ruthie stacked. I finished my homework, watched an hour or so of TV, and by ten-thirty I was ready for bed. I know that's early, but games take a lot out of me.

I lay in my narrow bed, drifting. I could hear the wind howling outside my window, and see the snow piling up on the sill. Lucky to be indoors, in a safe, warm apartment.

Lucky to have such a good mother and sisters, even if the former was beginning to exhibit the food preferences of a bovine, and the latter had the personalities of Godzilla and Rodan.

Lucky to have been in a zone. Some people don't even score forty-three points in their wildest dreams.

Lucky to have Janey for a girlfriend. Very, very lucky.

I lay there and reminded myself of how lucky I was in so many ways, and tried to be thankful and not think about playing basketball for my country in Europe.

Probably I wouldn't have been able to play at that level anyway. It was very possible I would have just made a fool of myself and ended up warming the bench. I was much better off here in Granham, where I was a high school hero, with everything going for me.

It took me a long time to fall asleep.

CHAPTER THREE

When the Sutherlands first began inviting me to dinner, I hesitated. They were so well off, upper class, and super educated that I felt intimidated. Also, I didn't know exactly how they felt about my dating their daughter, and I was afraid that they were inviting me over for all the wrong reasons.

My mom didn't like the idea, either. She suspected I was trying to get away from her vegetarian cooking, and on a deeper level I think the idea of my going somewhere for free dinners bothered her. The last thing she ever wanted was for any of us to take charity. She had fought her whole life against that. But in the end she agreed that once every two weeks was okay, provided that Janey came to our house every so often in return.

Janey's mother is a gracious, good-natured woman, who speaks five languages and got her M.D. before she turned twenty-seven. I don't know where she gets her energy from; she works a full day, seems to do most of the cooking and cleaning around her house, and somehow also has the time every week to read three or four thick books that it would take me a whole summer to plow through. All in all she's probably the second smartest and most capable person I've ever met in my life.

Her husband is the first. Anne Sutherland is an amazing intellectual, but she's not interested in less sophisticated things. Edward Sutherland is a junk-food junkie of information — he seems to know absolutely everything about everything, from the latest advances in medicine to obscure historical anecdotes to the hot local gossip. I was amazed to discover that he knew the pro basketball teams as well as I did. Once I started talking about Granham's chances in the county tournament, and Edward Sutherland almost knocked me off my seat by starting to analyze the strengths and weaknesses of different teams in our area.

Three nights after the Eisenhower game I was sitting at their elegant dinner table, happily devouring a plate of grilled lamb chops and listening to him tell an anecdote about the War of 1812. To tell you the truth, I didn't know anything about the War of 1812 except the year it was fought. Judging by the attention she was paying her dinner, Janey also didn't have much to contribute. Anne Sutherland probably knew a little bit more than we did, but I noticed she wasn't saying too much, either.

Watching Edward Sutherland go on easily about the battle of Tippecanoe, I couldn't help comparing him to my memory of my father. The two men actually have one very real link, forged long before I met and started going out with Janey. When my father collapsed from

24

his massive heart attack and they whisked him to the county hospital, Dr. Sutherland was the heart surgeon who tried to save his life.

I met him only once back then, when he came out and gave my mother and me the bad news. I guess he could have had some nurse or junior doctor do it, but he's not a man to pass the buck.

When I started going out with Janey and she introduced me to him, I knew I had met him before, but it took me a little while to place his face. When I finally did, I wondered if he remembered me. We'd only met once, under terribly strained circumstances, nearly six years ago, and he had dozens of patients every week. So even though I knew he had a photographic memory, I was very surprised when, one day when we were alone together on his front porch overlooking Blackfoot Lake, he said, "Jim, could I ask you a serious — and very difficult — question?"

"Yes, sir." I thought he was going to ask if Janey and I were fooling around.

Dr. Sutherland looks a little bit like Jack Nicklaus. But as he looked at me that day, his usually relaxed and smiling face was tight and serious. "Do you blame me for not being able to save your father's life?"

I almost fell into the lake. "No, sir. Not at all. No one could have done more."

"I hope that's true." I had never heard him express anything even close to self-doubt before. We stood side by side, looking out at the lake. "When I was your age,

I used to think of doctors — especially surgeons — as gods," he said. "With the power of life and death. To be very honest, that's one reason why I went to medical school. I'm a bit of an egomaniac and I wanted that power. Now that I am a surgeon, I realize just how great the limitations are on what we can and can't do."

"I never blamed you for a minute," I told him. "And neither has my mom."

"There's a cruel joke about doctors . . ." he continued. "That we bury our failures. It's not true. I think I can close my eyes and look back through my twenty-year career and tell you about every single patient I've lost." He was silent for a long minute, and I wondered what he was thinking about. "Your father fought like hell," he finally said in a low voice. "He never had a chance, but I fought and he fought. And I wanted you to know that."

Now, I sat there in the dining room, watching Edward Sutherland carve his lamb chops. His surgeon's hands wielded the serrated knife quickly and effortlessly, slicing the lamb off the bone as if it were an operation. The perfect father. The perfect husband. The almost perfect doctor. Occasionally, even he lost a patient. . . .

"So," he said, "you got quite a spread in the paper two days ago, Jim."

"I got hot for a while. We were lucky to win." When they talk about me, I always try to change the subject as quickly as possible. "These lamb chops are delicious. . . ."

"It didn't have anything to do with luck. He was in a zone," Janey said.

"Is that like being in the penalty box in a hockey game?" Anne Sutherland asked. She didn't know much about sports, but when we talked about it she felt compelled to contribute. Sometimes, I had the uncomfortable feeling that she was secretly making fun of us.

Janey rolled her eyes. "No," Edward Sutherland told his wife. "It means he suddenly elevated his game to another dimension."

"I see. Is entering the zone a psychological or a physiological phenomenon?"

"I can't say. I've never been in one," he admitted. "Jim is the only person at this table who has."

They all looked at me. How do you describe being in a zone to two brilliant doctors? "I guess, more than anything, it's . . . spiritual. Like when you dance to music and you're having a really great time, sometimes you forget you're dancing . . . and it's like you're inside the music. . . ." I stopped, feeling foolish.

There was a bit of a silence.

"Is an end zone a kind of zone?" Anne Sutherland asked.

"Mom," Janey said loudly, exasperated.

"I'm just kidding, dear." And then she looked at me. "Being in a zone does sound like fun. Do you think I could ever get into one?"

"No, ma'am," I said honestly. "I think you're too smart."

"You mean I'm too analytical to stop listening to music and just dance from inside of it?"

"I don't know," I mumbled. "Maybe."

"You're wrong there," Edward Sutherland told me. "Get any woman on a dance floor when the right song is playing, and she loses the intellectual function entirely."

At that point Janey and her mother began calling him a sexist, and the dinner conversation kind of broke down into accusations and witty defenses. I was glad to stop talking about zones and just concentrate on my lamb chops.

After dinner, we went into the study to watch a figure-skating competition that Janey wanted to see on TV. Her mother, who is easily bored, soon left, and Janey surprised me by inventing an excuse and following her out. Dr. Sutherland and I watched for a few minutes alone. Finally, he glanced over at me. "Beautiful stuff, but a tad boring."

I was glad he'd said it. "I thought Janey wanted to see it."

"As a matter of fact, I'm afraid we were manipulated into this . . . slightly awkward situation."

"She didn't really want to watch?"

"Do you mind if I switch it off?" He turned the TV off. "Now then. This is a bit awkward for me, but like you, I'm not exactly a free agent where the machinations of Janey and her mother are involved."

I waited.

"My daughter is a very observant young woman," Dr.

Sutherland said. "In this, she probably takes after her mother, who could have taught Sherlock Holmes a few tricks. I must tell you that acute powers of observation are not necessarily a desirable quality in one's girl-friend or wife. They occasion all sorts of awkward questions."

"I don't understand. What questions?"

"My daughter is under the impression that you've been 'turning something over and over,' as she puts it, for the better part of a week. And she says you won't talk about it with her. So she thought a father figure should have a go at you."

"It's nothing."

"Come, come," he said. "Once a woman gets a scent, she follows it through field and forest like a hound. Better to just come clean."

"It's personal."

"Well, I certainly don't mean to invade your privacy. It's nothing to do with Janey, then, and how you feel about her? Or about her eccentric parents?"

"Oh, no sir. Nothing like that at all."

"And you're sure you wouldn't feel better talking about it? In confidence, of course."

I stood up and stuck my hands in my pockets. "It's really nothing. I'm amazed Janey could even tell that I've been thinking about it so much. It's just that . . . I had a nice invitation that I had to turn down."

"That's always an unpleasant thing to have to do. A social invitation?"

"Kind of."

"An educational opportunity?"

"You could say that also."

Dr. Sutherland smiled at me. "Jim, I'm afraid we're not making much headway."

So I broke down and told him about the offer to play in Europe, and how I had said no, and why. "I guess more than anything it's that I've never had a chance to travel . . . even around this country . . . let alone Europe . . . and it would be an opportunity to make friends with the very best basketball players in the world my age . . . so I've had a hard time putting it out of my mind."

"Did you tell your mother about it?"

"No."

"May I ask why not?"

"It would have made her feel guilty about something that's not her fault."

He nodded. "It sounds like you made a tough but very sensible decision. You're a remarkably mature fellow. Now, shall we go find Janey and my wife?"

And then, when we were all set to leave the room, I kind of surprised myself by asking: "Dr. Sutherland, it's normal for a person to doubt himself sometimes, isn't it? And to feel unsure about the reasons he does things?"

He stopped at the doorway and looked at me. "I'm not sure what you're asking."

"Just . . . that I don't know how I'd do if I went over there and played with the best guys in the world my age."

Dr. Sutherland stepped back in from the door. As we studied each other's faces in the wood-paneled study, I flashed back to the day he had told me that he remembered each one of the patients he had lost during his twenty-year career. And I thought that if even a man as nearly perfect as Dr. Sutherland had self-doubts and found the courage to show his weaknesses to me, then . . . perhaps . . . he might be able to advise me about my own fears.

For a moment, I almost told him the complete truth, but then I heard myself back away. "And I guess I'm disappointed because of the situation with my family and the store and all, I won't have the chance to find out how I stack up against those other guys."

He put his arm on my shoulder. "I've only seen you play a few times, but I know enough about basketball to feel sure you'll have other chances to play at a very high level. And to travel and see the world, too. This time, it sounds as if you didn't have much choice."

"Thanks. Thanks for talking to me."

A little later I said good-bye to the Sutherlands and walked home. It felt good to have talked with Dr. Sutherland. One problem with not having a father is you feel you're missing out on a lot of conversations. Janey's father had said the exact things I wanted to hear. For the first time since the Eisenhower game, I felt as if I had put the whole international competition thing behind me.

I began to jog. There's nothing quite like running through new-fallen powder at night. Streetlights lighted my path — I could just see the outlines of the curb beneath the blanket of white snow. My boots made muffled thuds, and occasionally sank into drifts so that it felt like running on sand.

Good to have put things behind me. Arms pumping. Knees rising and falling. I might not have been able to play at that level of competition, anyway. In any case, I'd find out how I stacked up as a hoop player when I went to college. Breathing the icy air in deep gulps. Now I could concentrate on finishing the school year, helping out at the hardware store, and having a great summer with Janey. . . .

I got home after ten. Usually my mom goes to bed early, and I was surprised to find her waiting up in the living room. She was sitting in her favorite rocker, reading the comics from the morning's newspaper.

"Hi," I said.

She lowered the paper. "Why didn't you tell me?"

I started to reply, and then closed my mouth and we just looked at each other. Her eyes were blurry and red with fatigue, and she looked older than thirty-eight. She stood up and walked close to me. "What do you think I've worked so hard for all these years?" she asked very softly. "For myself?"

"I don't know what you mean. . . ."

"Mr. Griffin called from Los Angeles today — got me when I was alone in the hardware store. He started off apologizing for interfering in our personal business. But he said he wanted to find out what was really going on. Of course, I didn't have the slightest idea what he was talking about."

"Why torture ourselves with things we can't afford to do?" I asked her. "Anyway, I'm sure they've already replaced me with some other player."

"Mr. Griffin is holding your spot for you. For a few more days. I like this Mr. Griffin. We had a nice long talk."

"I liked him, too, but Mom, be real. . . ."

And then something about the way my mother was looking at me made me stop arguing. The corners of her lips moved upward in a very faint smile, and her red and blurry eyes suddenly began to glow. She stepped forward, put her hands on my shoulders, stood up on her tiptoes, and kissed me very gently on the forehead. I had never seen her smile quite like that before. "My baby is going to represent the United States of America," she whispered proudly.

I pulled back, almost out of her reach. She seemed surprised that I moved away. Her hands clung to my shoulders and we stood there for several seconds, looking into each other's eyes. "There's no way I can go," I said. "You know that as well as I do. It just doesn't make sense. June is our busiest month."

"Yes. Carrie will have to help me. Ruthie, too."

"Ruthie and Carrie don't know anything about the stock. And they're too young!"

"They're old enough to start learning. Jimmy, I want you to go." She read something in my eyes then, and her hands fell to her sides. "What is it?"

I stepped back, away from her searching gaze. "You talked to Mr. Griffin. . . . The team he's putting together will be the best players in this whole country. They're going to play against the best in the entire world. Mom . . ." My body shivered as my voice trembled and suddenly swung wildly out of control. "It doesn't make any sense. It's just a crazy dream."

"What is? Tell me what?"

So, finally, I said it out loud. "I can't play at that level. I never have . . . and I know I can't. So my job is here, helping my family."

My mother — the toughest person I've ever known — nodded slowly, as if she was reluctantly giving up something. "I see. Mr. Griffin and I were on entirely the wrong track." And then, in a very different voice, "Yes, of course I can use your help in the store. It will make June a much easier month. Now, I should say good night because I'm very tired."

"Good night," I mumbled back.

But instead of heading to her bedroom, she just stood there, looking at me.

Seconds ticked away.

Finally I asked her, "Aren't you going to bed?"

"Yes," she said. "Yes, I am. Yes . . . Jim, I know you were young and you may not remember your father's last year very clearly . . ."

"Mom, please . . ."

"He was a brave and strong man. But at the end of his life, between debts and his health . . . fear took hold of him. It was painful to watch . . . a man gripped by fear

34

like that . . . all he could tell me was that we were going to fail . . . we were going to lose the store . . . he was peering into an abyss . . . he never really confronted it. . . ."

"Don't you call me a coward," I ordered her. "I'm just trying to be real, for both of our sakes."

"All right," she answered. "You be real. I'm very tired. Remember to turn off all the lights before you go to bed. Good night." Then she went into her bedroom and closed the door, leaving me all alone in the silent apartment.

CHAPTER FOUR

Spring in Minnesota is worth waiting for. In a few warm weeks the white blanket of snow melts down into mud and winter grass. Ice-covered lakes crack and thaw till blue water once again ripples in the wind. Bony black limbs of trees that have hunched naked and shivering against the blasts of winter for seven months are suddenly softened by green buds. And then the first cheerful crocuses, violets, and daffodils burst open in tiny explosions of color in Granham Park.

A month or two later Janey and I stepped over dozens of budding flowers as we followed the stream that runs through the center of the park and feeds into Otter Lake. We were both in shorts and T-shirts, and I have to admit I spent more time looking at Janey than I did admiring the spring foliage. She looks cute all year long, but on this warm spring day with the sappy smell from trees hanging in the air and flies buzzing above the rush of the stream, Janey's white shorts and light pink T-shirt made her a bit hard to resist. I controlled myself for about twenty minutes while we made our way through the crowded center of the park, but when we came to a secluded spot, I grabbed her.

I guess she didn't mind too much, because she grabbed me right back. We wrestled and laughed and kissed a bit more. It's a nice feeling to roll around in fresh spring grass beneath a blue sky with a girl you love. I recommend it highly. To tell the truth — I'd better lower my voice — it might even beat playing basketball.

We ended up on our backs, picking out shapes in the few clouds. Janey's head was cushioned on my chest and strands of her long hair blew across my face. I saw two clouds, side by side, that looked like an automobile hitting a cow. Janey said that that was about the least romantic thing she'd ever heard, and that the clouds looked to her like a fawn grazing on a patch of clover. "What about the next one, over there?" she asked.

"Should I be honest or make up something sweet and romantic?"

"I would never tell you to make up something," she answered. "Although if it happened to remind you of something romantic, that would be nice."

I may not be the brightest guy in Minnesota but I got the message. "It looks like . . . a bouquet of roses sprouting from a heart."

She giggled and then punched me lightly on the shoulder. "Much too corny, try again."

"Okay, it looks like . . . a pair of lips kissing a basketball."

"That's disgusting. Who would ever kiss a basketball?"

"I would, if I thought it would help my shots go in."

"One more chance," she said. "Be real honest."

"It looks like an airplane taking off . . ." I began, and regretted it immediately.

"Great. End of game," she muttered.

"Janey, it does look like one of those old-fashioned airplanes. See, there are two wings . . . I was just being honest."

"Airplanes are the last thing I want to talk about right now," she sulked. "Just keep quiet and let me rest my head on your chest."

So we lay there for a few minutes. She shut her eyes. I kept mine open and watched her breathe through lips that were parted a tiny bit. Finally she opened her eyes and watched me watching her. "What are you thinking about?" she wanted to know.

"You," I said truthfully.

"Good answer. And what else?"

"The other nine guys . . . my teammates who I'm going to meet in Los Angeles. They're the best players in the entire country."

"So what?"

Now that I was definitely going, it was a little bit easier for me to talk about my doubts. "Do you know how big a country this is? How many guys my age play basketball? I hope I don't end up just sitting the bench."

"That's if they even let you into the gym at all," she said.

"I knew I could count on you for sympathy."

"You're gonna do just fine," she whispered in my ear. "Maybe you won't be the very best, like you are here in

Granham. But they wouldn't have asked you to come if they didn't think you deserved it. And you're going to have a wonderful time in Los Angeles and Italy. You're gonna see the Colosseum, and the Forum. Let me see your hand."

"Oh, don't start with that stuff. You've already seen my palm a hundred times. There's nothing new there."

"What do you know about palm reading?" She took my hand and tilted it so that my palm caught the spring sunlight.

"What do you see?"

"It's dirty," she said, frowning.

"Very impressive psychic ability. Anything else?"

"Not really." But she kept looking at it as if she saw something there she didn't exactly like. And then she kissed the center of my palm and let go of it.

"What did you see?" I asked.

"Nothing."

"I saw that it was something. Come on. If I put up with this nonsense, you should at least tell me the truth."

"Okay," she said. "It was really nothing. But I think . . . maybe . . . you're going to have a rough trip."

"Rough how?"

"I don't know. Really, it was nothing. Let it go, Jimmy."

"Okay. You're the one who wanted to tell my fortune. I should get home soon."

"Are you sure you don't want me to come with you to the airport to say good-bye?"

"Not with my mother there. And all the other travelers. I'd rather say good-bye here."

She kissed me on the ear. "Okay. Good-bye." And then I got two on the lips. "And good-bye and good-bye." She stood up, and I did also. We started walking back the way we had come, following the stream out of the park. The greenish-blue water of the swollen stream glided by us, here and there foaming white over black rocks. Janey broke the silence as we left the park. "If you meet any pretty Italian girls, will you do me a favor?"

"Sure. What?"

"Tell them you're sorry, but you don't speak their language."

Janey's always been a tiny bit jealous, and I like to tease her about it. "I've actually been studying a few words."

"Like what?"

"Vuoi prendere un caffè insieme?"

"What does that mean?"

"Would you like to get a cup of coffee with me?"

"You don't even like coffee."

"Well, what about you? With me gone, I know you're gonna meet all these handsome, brilliant guys."

She looked up and down the empty street. "Where are they? I'll settle for even one."

We were nearing the corner where we both knew we would say good-bye. She lived to the north. My house was to the south. "Guys from rich families." I took her hand. "Who own their own cars and don't need to work on weekends."

"But can they shoot three-point shots?" she asked. "Because I only go out with guys who can hit three-point shots."

"An outside touch is a gift," I told her.

We kissed one last time and stepped apart. We were still holding hands, reluctant to let go. "You have a good time over there," she said. "Score lots of points. Win a gold medal or a silver jockstrap or whatever prize they're giving out. Don't even look at any Italian girls. And come back soon."

"Okay," I promised. "I'd better go now."

"I love you," Janey said. It was the first time either of us had ever said it out loud. She looked scared when the three words popped out of her mouth. Before I could respond, she let go of my hand and hurried away without looking back.

I had packed that morning, and my suitcase and duffel bag were labeled with my home address and waiting by the door. Ruthie and Carrie insisted on carrying my luggage to the car for me, and giving me farewell hugs. "Good-bye, Garbage Breath," Ruthie said, hugging me.

"How about more respect for the only world-class athlete in the family?"

"Don't kiss me good-bye with your wormy lips," Carrie shouted, squirming away. "If you don't do well playing basketball in Italy, maybe you can learn to make pizza."

"Your big ears can be the mushrooms, and Ruthie's long nose can be the sausage."

"Mom, make him apologize. I don't have big ears."

"And my nose isn't long. . . ."

Mom and I got into the car and left the two monsters behind, with our neighbor, Mrs. Mills. It was about an hour's drive through farm country and past ponds and occasional large lakes to Minneapolis–St. Paul International Airport. Mom and I didn't talk too much along the way. I checked in, and they were already calling my flight so we hurried to the gate. "Any last-minute advice?" I asked her.

"Don't rush your shots."

I had to smile. Mom knows virtually nothing about basketball. "Okay. Is that it?"

"Wash behind your ears and put on clean underwear."

I could see the woman behind me in line smile as she overheard this advice. "Mom . . . don't embarrass me. . . ."

We were nearing the gate. "I don't need to give you any advice," she said. "You know what to do. Be a credit to your country and come home safe. I might even cook you some chicken."

"Okay, I'll come home."

"Ticket, please," a pretty airline worker said.

I gave her my ticket and gave my mother a hug and a kiss. Then I took my ticket back and headed in through the gate. I turned once and Mom was still standing right near the ticket counter, watching me walk away. She smiled and waved. I grinned and waved back, and then I walked onto the plane.

The fact that something as big as a 747 can actually rise off the ground into the clouds seems miraculous. I had the window seat, and I watched with my face almost pressed against the pane as we rolled down the runway, tilted up into thin air, and finally climbed toward the clouds. The ground was soon a patchwork quilt of green farms far beneath us. Cars shrank to matchbox size, and towns whirled by like pages from a giant map book. If you've flown a lot, this is probably old stuff to you, but seeing it all for the first time was one of the most exciting twenty minutes I can remember. Then we flew into a cloud and emerged above the cloud cover, out of sight of the ground below.

I read a *Sports Illustrated* and was surprised to find a short article about the tournament. It was being sponsored by an Italian tire manufacturer and a German candy company. According to the article, the American team, the Spanish team, the German team, and the Croatian team were the pretournament favorites. I guess the article had gone to press before the American team was picked, because they didn't list all ten players.

But the article did describe three players considered sure bets. I had heard or read about all of them before. Shawn Wright, a six-foot-five-inch center from Florida, was considered to be the best big man my age in the country. Jorge Gonzalez, a sophomore forward from Manhattan, was described as a shot-blocking machine with a superb inside game. And Augustus LeMay, a guard from Crenshaw High School in Los Angeles, was supposed to be the best all-around high school junior in the entire country.

There was a big picture of Augustus jamming a basketball. According to the article, he was six feet three inches tall — just two inches more than me — but in the photograph his hands and both wrists were clearly over the rim of the basket. On my best days, I can barely touch the rim. His head was shaved like Michael Jordan and his body was sleek and rippling with muscles. It only took one look at the photo to know that I had never played with or against anyone like this in Minnesota.

When I had read the article twice I watched a movie, managed a quick nap, and finished off a slightly stale ham sandwich. I was enjoying the trip and beginning to think that flying on airplanes was no big deal when we suddenly hit pockets of air turbulence above the Grand Canyon. The plane dropped steeply, like a roller coaster plunging down an almost vertical slope. I grabbed my armrests. We steadied for a few seconds, and then plummeted again, even more severely. FASTEN YOUR SEAT BELT lights blinked on. A stewardess walked down the aisle, checking on us.

She glanced at me, and I guess she could tell how nervous I was. "Is everything okay?" I asked her.

"This is just normal air turbulence. There's really nothing to worry about."

And then our plane dropped straight down, and I heard loud exclamations of surprise and alarm from other passengers. "Excuse me," the stewardess said, sounding just a bit alarmed herself. "I'd better go sit down."

The middle and aisle seats next to me were empty. It's amazing how alone you can feel on an airplane with dozens of other people in front and back of you. For the next ten minutes I half expected to die at any second. Plane travel no longer seemed like such a miracle, but rather like an encroachment on the divine power of flight. Birds can do it. Humans shouldn't. I sat there, head back, hands gripping the armrests, thinking of my mother and the two little monsters and Janey.

I made a vow that I would never ridicule fortune-telling again. No wonder Janey hadn't wanted to tell me what she saw in my palm. If she had, I might never have gotten on the plane. But as I sat there in the vibrating, pitching cabin, I couldn't help thinking that maybe staying in Minnesota would have been a good thing. I tried to relax and think of Janey's face, but the vibrating had gotten worse and all around me I could hear nervous whispering from other passengers. I said a little prayer.

Then a very calm male voice came over the intercom. "This is Captain Hawkins speaking. Sorry for the rough ride, folks. I've been talking to a few other planes in the area, and it sounds like things might be a little smoother for us at thirty thousand feet. So I'm going to take us up. Hang on and we should be out of this in two or three minutes."

I counted the seconds. Twice the plane lurched so

precipitously that I was sure we were going to break in half or explode. Somewhere in the back, by the restrooms, a baby started crying. A hundred seconds after the announcement, the vibrating lessened and then stopped. We lurched one or two final times, and then, as promised, our ride smoothed out. I held my breath and waited for things to get rocky again, but whatever Captain Hawkins had done had worked miraculously. The big plane was cruising quietly and peacefully above the cloud cover.

Bit by bit my body relaxed. The baby in the back of the plane stopped crying. I let go of the armrests, and felt a little bit silly for thinking that we were all doomed, and that the plane might break in half. It was probably a very normal thing to hit such air turbulence, and since I was an inexperienced flyer I had just made too much of it.

I grinned at how scared I had been, and remembered Janey and her prediction. If this was the rough trip she had predicted, it had not been all that bad. And now it was over. The sunny skies of southern California lay ahead.

CHAPTER FIVE

Los Angeles seemed to go on forever.

We flew in over a ring of snowcapped mountains, and then cruised for nearly half an hour high above a vast urban sprawl. There were skyscrapers and what looked like suburbs, green parks, and long streets that stretched mile after mile to a ribbon of brown beach and then the Pacific Ocean, sparkling endlessly off to the west.

After the scare above the Grand Canyon I was a bit worried about landing, but Captain Hawkins set us down gently on the landing strip. A few minutes later I was filing out the exit gate, scanning the two dozen or so waiting faces for one I knew.

Mr. Griffin spotted me just as I saw him. In Minnesota he had been wearing a suit, and I almost didn't recognize him in tan slacks and an olive-colored short-sleeved shirt. Many of the men and women waiting to meet passengers at the gate wore shorts and brightly colored T-shirts. I looked down at my jeans and flannel shirt — I could see that I would have to adjust to the California lifestyle.

"Welcome, Jimmy," he said as I got close. "Let's go find your luggage before somebody tries to walk away with it." He led me quickly toward an escalator. "Did you have a good flight?"

I hesitated. "It was an experience."

"The first of many on this trip."

Soon we were in his spanking-new convertible, speeding down a four-lane freeway. It was exactly what I had expected Los Angeles to be like — clear skies and picture-perfect eighty-five-degree weather. On either side of us, expensive-looking imported cars zipped through the sunshine. "First time in Los Angeles?" he asked.

"First time west of Omaha."

He glanced at my face to see if I was serious, and then chuckled. "We're a long way from Omaha. How's your mother, Jimmy?"

"Fine, sir."

"She's a great lady. We had a nice conversation. And you don't have to call me 'sir.'"

"She said she enjoyed talking to you, too . . ." I hesitated. "Should I call you Mr. Griffin or Terry or . . . ?"

"How about Coach?"

For some reason that surprised me, and at the same time made me very happy. "You're going to be coming with us?"

"You don't think I'd miss a trip to Italy? Chris McNeil and I are going to split the coaching duties. And we have two assistant coaches. I could have sent one of them to get you, but I've been trying to pick up our out-of-town players personally. We're all especially glad that you decided to come." He stuck out a long arm.

"Now this is West Los Angeles. The ocean's three miles that way. And UCLA, where we're going, is just another mile up the freeway."

"Are the other guys there already?"

"Most of them."

"I read about three of them in *Sports Illustrated*."

"Yeah, I saw that piece," Coach Griffin said. "You'll be rooming with one of those three. Shawn Wright."

"The big man."

"Plenty big, and still growing. We took early arrivals to a steak house last night, and damn if Shawn didn't eat half a cow. But he's a good guy. You'll get along."

We turned off the freeway, and drove through a college neighborhood with hip-looking stores and dozens of young people on the streets. "This is Westwood," Coach Griffin said. "And here's the entrance to UCLA."

It was an enormous and gorgeous campus. There was a giant new medical center, old and graceful Spanish-style buildings, and lush grass and pine trees everywhere. Signs pointed the way to the Wooden Center, named after the greatest college basketball coach in history, and Pauley Pavilion, where the UCLA basketball teams play their home games. We drove on, up a steep hill, to a complex of brand-new dorm buildings that looked out on tennis courts.

"These are the Sunset Canyon dorms, your home for the next week," Coach Griffin said. "You're in room twelve. Here's the room key, and here's an I.D. card that will get you into just about anywhere on campus. Try not to lose them."

He opened the back trunk and helped me get my two bags out. "Room twelve should be on the first floor. Do you need help carrying those inside?"

"No, sir. I mean, Coach. When do we all get together?"

He glanced at his watch. "We'll all meet in Pauley Pavilion in two hours for a get-acquainted session and maybe a little strategy. Wear street clothes and just follow the signs down the hill. After that, we'll go to dinner. Do you like Italian food?"

"Sure," I said, "as long as there's meat in the pasta sauce."

He gave me a curious look. "I think we can find something meaty enough for you. We're trying to get everyone used to Italian food before we go over there. See you in a couple of hours, Jim."

I lugged my suitcase and duffel bag into the dorm and found room twelve. Loud rap music was thumping inside the room. I knocked. No answer. I knocked much harder. The doorknob turned and a very tall and solidly built black kid of about my age, wearing just shorts and socks, stood looking down at me. He had a baby face, which was kind of strange for such an oak tree of a guy, and his head bobbed slightly back and forth to the rap music as he studied me.

I held out my right hand. "I think we're roommates. I'm Jimmy Doyle."

He studied me for a second more and then flashed a big and friendly smile and shook my hand. "Shawn Wright," he said. "C'mon in." I followed him into the room. A large picture window flooded the room with sunshine. There were two single beds, twin dressers, and two wooden desks. Shawn had already taken the bed by the window, so I tossed my stuff on the other one. He lay back down on his bed and watched me as I started to unpack. "Mind the music?"

I'm not crazy about rap, but I shook my head. "It's okay. Who is it?"

"Ice-T. You sure brought a lot of stuff."

"I guess maybe I overpacked. I've never been to California or Italy before."

"Me neither. I'm from Gainesville. What about you?"

"Granham. It's a small town in Minnesota."

"I didn't know anyone played basketball up there," he said with a grin. And then he surprised me by saying: "You're our starting shooting guard, right?"

"I don't know if I'm starting or not. I was just glad to make the team."

"The rumor is that you are. Or at least that it's your job till you lose it."

This was news to me. I began putting pairs of socks in the top drawer, conscious all the time that Shawn was watching me. I had packed more than a dozen pairs of socks, and it seemed to take forever to fish them out of the duffel and put them in the drawer.

"Man, how many feet you got?" Shawn finally asked.

"Like I said, maybe I overpacked. I haven't traveled much."

"Yeah, a couple of the guys were wondering about that. See, most of us know each other from playing in summer camps and all-star tournaments and stuff. But here you are, a starter, and nobody's ever heard of you before."

I didn't say anything. I wasn't about to tell a total stranger that I'd been helping my mom out in the hardware store every free moment I'd had for the past six years. So I just went on unpacking, sticking underwear in a drawer.

Shawn didn't let it go. "What have you been doing up there in Minnesota, mystery man?"

"Trying to stay warm."

He laughed. "Yeah, I hear you get a little snow now and then. But listen, you want that starting job, you're gonna have to prove yourself to some of the brothers." He inserted a headphone attachment into his tape player, put the headphones on, and grinned at me. "I can see you don't like my music. Do me a favor. Wake me up when it's time to head down to Pauley." And then Shawn rolled toward the window, stretched out, and went to sleep. His feet hung a few inches off the end of the bed.

I finished unpacking, took a hot shower, and went for a little walk. Within a few hundred yards of our dorm were more tennis courts than in all of Granham. Beyond the tennis courts I came to two of the largest swimming pools I had ever seen in my life, almost side by side. This corner of the campus was remarkably beautiful. The smell of pine filled the air, and fallen needles formed a brown carpet on the green grass.

I kept thinking of what Shawn had said about proving myself to the other guys. If they all knew each other, no wonder they were curious about the stranger from Minnesota. I couldn't figure out why our coaches had let word out that I was a starter, even before I arrived.

I woke Shawn with twenty minutes to spare. As a basketball player, Shawn had remarkable foot speed for a big man, but when it came to shaving, dressing, and combing his hair, he moved with the slowness of a true perfectionist. By the time we headed off down the hill together, the meeting time was only five minutes away.

We jogged side by side, and as we neared Pauley Pavilion I could feel my excitement rising. The nine best basketball players my age in the entire country were about to get their first look at me. Guys who could fly and jam. Guys with the inside moves and the outside touch. Future college stars and NBA prospects who knew what it was like to go into a zone just as well as I did. Or better. I glanced at my watch and speeded up a little, and soon Shawn and I were running quickly through the twilight.

The white concrete shell of Pauley Pavilion swam into view. We entered through the only open door and began making our way down, past rows of empty bleachers, toward the gleaming hardwood. I found out later that Pauley seats thirteen thousand people, which means the entire town of Granham wouldn't come close to filling it up. Completely empty, it looked even bigger. Despite our downhill run, we were a few minutes late.

The other guys had already arrived, and were gathered under one of the baskets.

They gave me appraising looks as Shawn and I walked up. I looked back at them, and an unexpected thought struck me. I don't usually classify people in racial terms, but in all of Granham there are only a dozen or so black families. Here in Los Angeles, on this team of all-stars, seven of the players were black. There was one other white guy, a slightly gawky-looking fellow who I guessed might be a backup forward, and a Latino with a crew cut who I took to be Jorge Gonzalez. As I made my way to the bench my black teammates, who were together, studied me with interest.

I looked back at them. All nine of my teammates were tall, appeared to be in great shape, and had the look of superb athletes, yet one of them immediately stood out from the crowd. Augustus LeMay looked just like his photo in *Sports Illustrated*. It wasn't just his shaved head à la Michael Jordan or the sleeveless black T-shirt that showed off his muscle definition . . . no, it was more than that, and in a way less than that. It was small things that are hard to catch: the way he sat — relaxed yet as ready to spring into action as a cat, the brightness of his eyes, the charisma that came from his total confidence in himself and played around him almost like a flame. From his shaved head and the gold earring in his left ear to his handsome and deeply chiseled features to the tips of his sneakers, he had future superstar written all over him.

I had read about him in the sports magazines for

years back in Granham, and wondered what it would be like to play in a backcourt with him, and whether I could keep up. And now here he was, in the flesh.

Coach McNeil had been speaking to the group, but he broke off as Shawn and I sat down at the end of the bench. "Okay, guys," he said, "we're all here now. This is Shawn, our center. . . ." Shawn raised his long right arm and lazily waved it. "And Jimmy from Minnesota, who can shoot the lights out at guard." Again, curious eyes swept over me. "Now, we'd better get this meeting going. We don't want to miss our dinner reservation or we'll end up at McDonald's."

"Hey, that'd be okay," one of the guys called out. He was a little chunky for a basketball player, and he had a fade haircut that angled steeply down at the side of his scalp.

"No it would not," Coach McNeil said. "No fast food on this trip. Nothing greasy. Nothing fried. You can eat as much as you want, but it's got to be healthy. I want you to order a salad with every lunch and every dinner." There were groans. "You'll love the salads in Italy," he said, trying to drum up enthusiasm. "The tomatoes explode in your mouth, and arugula will make you forget all about American lettuce."

"I don't eat tomatoes or lettuce," the same guy who had cut in before said. "That's rabbit food."

Coach Griffin answered him from the bench. "Thompson, you can eat what you want at home. But while you're on this team you'll eat healthy and enjoy it. Okay?"

55

"I'll eat it but I don't think I'll enjoy it."

"I know you're just kidding around," Coach McNeil said to him. "But I'm glad this happened because it lets me make an important point. In the next month, you guys are going to be exposed to media attention like you never saw before. The first press conference will be tomorrow, at noon."

There was an excited buzz among my teammates. "Who's gonna be there?" they wanted to know.

"Newspapers and TV stations, both local and national. And after tomorrow, the attention will be constant. Questions. Pictures. Inside stories. And in Italy it won't let up — it'll get even more intense. We're the favorites in this tournament — they're dubbing us the 'Teen Dream Team' — and I guarantee you that every single reporter there is going to want to get an angle on 'The Dream.' Do you know what that means?"

There was silence. "I got to shut up and eat tomatoes and a-rug-jug-la," the chunky kid said gloomily. A couple of guys chuckled.

"Arugula," Coach McNeil corrected him with a smile. "And it means more than that. It means if you step out of line, fight, get drunk, get caught with drugs, fool around with girls, or mess up in any way, it's gonna be splashed all over the world press. Now if that happens, we'll send you back to America on the first plane. We're bringing ten of you — we only need five to play. But even worse than sending you home will be that you'll get a reputation as a troublemaker. And a rep like that will follow you . . . stick to you. Recruiters will know it, college coaches will hear about it . . . so don't let it happen. We want this to be good for your futures, not bad. Got it?"

A few of us nodded.

"Say yes or no."

There was a chorus of yesses. "Okay then, I'm hungry." Coach McNeil glanced at his watch. "Terry, anything to add?"

"Just two things," Coach Griffin said, standing up and walking to the front. "First, it's not enough to just keep yourself in line. From now on, for the next four weeks, we're one big family. Which means we watch out for each other the way we would watch out for our brothers. Help each other. Watch each other's backs. If one of our brothers fails in some way, we all share the blame."

He paused, to let the words sink in. "Second, about that press conference tomorrow. How many of you have ever been at a press conference?"

Half of my teammates raised their hands.

"All right then, let me give you some advice. Don't get too deep. If they ask you how the team looks, say, 'We're gonna try our best, but it's gonna be tough all the way.' When they ask you whom you admire most in the world, say your father or the president. If they ask you what you do in your spare time, say, 'I just try to prepare myself mentally and physically so that I can do a good job of representing the United States of America.'"

A couple of the guys snickered.

"Terry has played college and pro ball and he's giving you very good advice," Coach McNeil told us. "If you're always positive and humble, you'll never get burned by the press. Try to say something sassy or critical, and I guarantee it'll come back to haunt you. Now let's get some dinner."

We walked half a mile to a big Italian restaurant in Westwood. During the walk, Shawn told me enthusiastically that the European sponsors of the tournament and the American Junior Athletic Association had given us a generous training budget, so we could order anything we wanted. I had a salad, a giant slab of meat lasagna, and two orders of garlic bread.

Ray Thompson, the short and chunky wise guy, was sitting next to me. He entertained our whole table by making fun of Coach Griffin's advice on how to deal with the press. "Now if they ask what kind of lady you like to date, you don't say a fox. You don't talk about legs or boobs. You say," and he imitated Coach Griffin's voice, " 'It's an honor to represent the United States of America, and I'm preparing myself mentally and physically for fifty years of marriage with a woman just like my coach's dear old grandmother.' "

Coach Griffin, at the next table, heard this. I thought he might get mad, but he only laughed along with the rest of us.

Encouraged, our team comedian continued. "If they ask you what you do to stay psyched up, you don't tell them, 'Coach is kicking our butts in practice every day.' No, you say, 'Sir, playing in this tournament is the honor of my young life, and every time I walk onto the court I feel so full of red, white, and blue spirit I almost pop like a firecracker on the Fourth of July.'" He looked at Coach Griffin. "Did I get that right?"

"Perfect," Coach Griffin responded, shaking his head. "Remind me to muzzle you before the press conference."

We walked back together and I felt good, after a big and delicious dinner and a lot of laughs. The coaches said good-bye to us for the night, and the ten of us headed up the hill to our dorms. I trailed a little behind and was surprised to see our star, Augustus LeMay, drop back to be with me. "Hey," I said, "we didn't get to meet. I'm Jimmy Doyle, from Minnesota." I held out my hand.

He studied my face, and didn't take my hand. "Yeah, I know who you are." His earring gleamed in the illumination of a streetlight. "You're the guy who screwed me and my homeboy over."

"What are you talking about? I never met you before in my life."

"Tomorrow morning," he said. "In the gym. You got anything to show, I'll be right there, watching."

And then, before I could reply, he speeded up and was soon out of sight along the curving road.

CHAPTER SIX

At a little before eight o'clock, all ten of us assembled in the vast and empty gym.

Practice uniforms and sweats had been brought to
our rooms early that morning, so we were all wearing
identical blue shorts and red-and-white shirts with *USA*
on the front and *Junior World Team* on the back. Our
coaches hadn't arrived yet, but a double rack of basketballs had been set out, so we began to shoot around. It
was an interesting moment. We all pretended that we
were just taking our own shots, but what was really going on was a lot of covert glances as we got our first
look at our teammates.

In between my own ten- and fifteen-footers, I
watched Augustus LeMay and a guard named Jamal
Stokes, who was Augustus's roommate and seemed to
be his friend. They had a little shooting competition —
one would try to take a quick jumpshot while the other
played defense.

Augustus had a great stroke — the ball came off his
fingers effortlessly and with perfect rotation. I could tell
from one glance that he and the net were old friends. He
blocked two of Jamal's shots, but he sank his own with-

out any apparent effort. He was able to move his hands so quickly that his jumpshots were in the air almost before Jamal could react. One. Swish. Two. Swish. Three. Swish. Our coaches were walking down the aisle and it was clear that practice was about to start, so instead of taking a final jumpshot, Augustus faked going up, dribbled the ball in past Jamal, launched himself into the air, and jammed it home.

It was a tough first practice. Everyone was anxious to make a good impression so nobody slacked off. By the time we were done with drills and running some basic plays, we were all breathing hard. I was surprised at how many of the plays were designed for me. Picks. Screens and double screens to free me up in the corner. It became pretty clear that I was in fact going to be one of the starters, and that the coaches had a lot of confidence in my shooting.

We took a fifteen-minute break, and then came back on the floor for our first scrimmage. "We're not looking for you to hotdog it," Coach McNeil told us. "We scouted every single one of you so we already know you can play. Today we just want to see you move the ball around, work for good shots, and show us your defense."

They broke us down into two teams, and it was pretty obviously the starters against the second string. Augustus and I were the starting guards. My big roommate Shawn was our center. Jorge Gonzalez was one of our forwards and an intense guy from Detroit whom everyone called "Stinger" was the other. They called him

"Stinger" because once he got around you on the base-line he would "sting" you — he was a great finisher who would take the ball right to the hoop.

We huddled for a minute before the start. I looked around at my teammates — these four perfectly condi-tioned athletes were worlds away from the good-hearted Granham goofs I usually carried through games back home. Shawn said, "Nobody selfish. Work it in-side. Let's bust our butts and show up these suckers!"

As we ran out onto the floor, Augustus LeMay ran by me and whispered, "Put up or shut up."

"What's your problem?" I whispered back. "We don't even know each other. . . ." And then the game started.

I have to admit, it was probably the worst forty-five minutes of basketball I have ever played. My passes were intercepted. I had three shots rejected, and the ones that made it over or around the defense were, for the most part, bricks. Ray Thompson, the comedian from the previous night's dinner, was all business as he guarded me. I guess he wanted my starting job. When I moved without the ball, he anticipated my cuts. When I tried to drive, he always seemed to have position in front of me.

On offense he was a little piston powering their team's fast break, bringing the ball up quickly time and time again, penetrating, and then finding the right dish inside or the perfect kick-out pass. Ray kept kicking the ball out to a streak shooter named Hayes, who got hot and swished three long jumpshots in a row. I got the feeling that Hayes also wanted my starting job and was showing our coaches his stuff. He had quick hands and superb body control, and every time he drained a long shot he'd raise both arms and give a yell of triumph, as if to make sure everyone gave him full credit.

This was a whole different level of basketball than even the county championship game back in Minnesota, and I felt as if I was drowning. My lowest moment came when Jorge Gonzalez made a steal and threw me a long lead pass on a breakaway. I took it to the hoop unopposed, but I guess I was conscious that two of their players were on my heels because somehow I missed the wide-open layup. My shot rolled around the rim and out.

Every basketball player probably blows a layup at one time or another, but coming on top of all my other missed shots and errors, the miss completely deflated me for a minute. I stood with my hands on my hips, staring at the floor and shaking my head.

"Get back in the game, Doyle!" Coach McNeil shouted.

That yell got me going again. As I hustled back down to play defense, I passed Augustus LeMay. He gave me a disgusted look and shook his head slightly, as if to ask, "What are you even doing out on this floor?"

Finally, mercifully, the scrimmage ended. The starters lost by a couple of baskets, which was almost certainly my fault. The rest of the first stringers had played just fine. Augustus LeMay had scored more than twenty points, and he had shone with equal brilliance on both offense and defense. I had never seen anyone who moved like him, with or without the ball. All during that long scrimmage, as I struggled with my game, I had been very conscious of him gliding easily up and down the court. I had always thought of myself as a pretty good all-around player — watching him, for the first time, I felt like just a slow and awkward streak shooter brought in from the boondocks. Augustus LeMay had a complete game, from passing to defense, from shooting to blocking, and now as we gathered on the bench he was looking right at me with contempt.

"Okay, guys, that was a start," Coach McNeil said. "We've got about forty-five minutes till the press conference. You can stay here and shoot or you can hustle back to your rooms and shower. But I want all of you right here at one."

About half the guys headed up the aisle to go back to the dorms. I started to follow them, but Coach McNeil grabbed my arm. "Hang out for a second."

I stood there nervously, waiting for him to speak. It seemed as if all my worst fears back in Granham had proven true. I couldn't play with these guys. On the court, I could see a couple of them who had chosen to remain taking shots. Augustus LeMay sank a long swish. "Do you want to send me back to Minnesota?" I asked Coach McNeil.

"Don't talk crazy," he said. "I know it was a little rough for you out there, but I've seen a lot of basketball in my life and there's no doubt in my mind that you can play at this level. It's just going to be an adjustment. Okay?"

I nodded, and mumbled "I'll try" without too much conviction. "Thanks."

He slapped me on the back. "Don't thank me. We brought you out here because we need you. I gotta go take care of a few things now. See you at the press conference."

Coach McNeil walked away, and I started to follow him. Then I changed my mind. There was something I had to do, and there was no sense putting it off. I turned and walked toward the court. Augustus, his friend Jamal, Stinger, Ray, and Shawn were shooting around. I walked straight over to Augustus. He was squaring up to shoot, but when he saw me coming he lowered the ball to hip height.

"Can we talk for a second?" I asked him.

His face remained expressionless.

"What do you have against me?"

"You don't belong here," he said.

I was thinking the same thing, but the fact that he said it out loud, in front of the other players, made me angry. "You can't say that. You don't know me or what I'm capable of yet."

"I saw you play. If that's what you were doing today."

The other guys had stopped shooting and were standing around, watching us. I controlled my temper with an effort. "I know I looked bad this morning, but you started with me last night after dinner, before you ever saw me take a shot. Tell me why?"

He took a small step closer to me. "Okay, I will," he said. "Devonne Saunders."

"Who's that?"

"Like you expect me to believe you don't know?"

"You can believe whatever you want. I've never heard of him."

"He's the guy who should be the other starting guard," Augustus LeMay said. "But they dropped him to put some whitebread on our team. That's you, Mr. Minnesota."

"I am white and I'm from Minnesota. So what? I still don't get it."

"It's just that I don't have much patience with the hypocritical jive that says a team representing America has to have some rich, blond-haired stiff who wouldn't last five minutes on any playground in this city."

I almost answered back about being rich. But I figured it was none of his or anyone else's business that I had spent practically all of my free time since grade school helping my mom try to dig our family out of debt and put three meals on the table. "You're talking from ignorance," I told him, and started away.

A few of the other guys whistled. Augustus dropped the ball and came after me. "Ignorance? Say what?"

"Leave it alone, bro," Shawn advised him.

"The man just called me ignorant." He stepped very close. "Maybe you didn't know what you were saying, Mr. Minnesota?"

I saw that he was giving me an out. But what he had said about my poor performance had tapped into my

66

worst fears about not belonging there. "Ignorant or just plain stupid."

He put his chest right up against mine. "Don't push me, man. Get off this court before I throw you off."

My fingers folded into fists. "You can try if you want."

I sensed that deep down he wasn't looking for a fight, and I certainly wasn't, either, but it had reached the point where neither one of us could back down. He shoved me with his chest, and I pushed him back. There were a few heart-stopping seconds of glaring back and forth, and then he shoved me again, a little harder, and I lost all self-control and swung at him.

Augustus wasn't expecting the punch. He raised his left arm to block it, but the blow glanced off his elbow and caught him in the nose hard enough to knock him backward. For a shocked second, time froze in the empty vastness of Pauley Pavilion. Augustus wiped his nose with the back of his wrist, and blood showed clearly. Then he stepped forward and hit me twice, bam, bam, first on the side of the head and then in the stomach. I found myself lying on my back on the gym floor.

"Get up," Augustus said, standing over me. "Come on, Minnesota. GET UP!"

As I struggled to my feet, Shawn stepped in between us. "That's enough."

"Stay out," Augustus growled at him.

"I'm already in," Shawn growled back. And then, in a different voice, he said to Augustus, "You don't

wanna be doing this. We're gonna need you in Italy."
Then Shawn put his massive arms around my shoulders
and started dragging me away.

I tried to shake free, but he held me. "Let it go," he
said. "Don't keep fighting me. I gotta take you out of
here." It was hard to resist this gentle giant who was
dragging me along with the force of a tractor. "I can explain some things to you, later on. . . ." By now he had
dragged me about fifteen or twenty feet. "C'mon, man,
just let it go. . . ."

My head was throbbing from the punch, and I felt
dizzy. I let Shawn drag me off the court and somehow
he got me up the stairs and out of Pauley Pavilion. I
barely remember walking back up the hill to my dorm.
Shawn left me for a while on my bed, and returned with
some ice wrapped up in a towel. "It's a shame about
your eye. You're gonna look bad for a day or two."

I held the ice to my head. "A shame for who?"

"Coach is not gonna like it. Now, here's what you
say. You were in a hurry to get to that press conference
and you walked into a door coming back to our room."

"Why should I lie? He started with me! Everybody
saw it."

"You swung first — hit him in the face. Up till then it
was just pushing and shoving. And if you want to hang
with us, you won't go whispering to the coach about
what happened when he wasn't there."

"I wish you had let us settle it."

"Let me clue you in," Shawn said. "You don't stand a
chance in the world fighting Augie."

"I'm not afraid of him."

"I didn't say you were. But you don't know a thing about fighting. If you take on Augie, you're just asking for a beating."

The ice throbbed against the side of my face. The truth has a way of registering, even when you're angry and in pain. "What does he have against me, anyway? Who's this Devonne Saunders?"

"You really don't know?"

"I never heard his name before today."

"Devonne's one of the best guards in America. I've played against him a few times and he's got a sweet game. He lives in L.A. and I guess the coaches talked to him about coming as our starting guard, and then something happened and they took you instead."

"Why didn't they bring both of us?"

"All I know is that they offered him a place and then they took the offer away, and you came."

"And this Devonne guy is Augustus's friend?"

"His cousin," Shawn said. "They grew up together and they didn't have what you would call easy childhoods. That made them close. It also gave Augie some strong opinions on who he does and does not want as friends. If I were you I wouldn't call him or any of the brothers ignorant."

"I didn't mean it as a . . ."

"I know you didn't. But I still wouldn't say it again." He glanced at the clock next to his bed. "I gotta get down to that press conference. Know what I would do if I were you?"

"What?"

"Stay here. You don't want anyone taking pictures of your face right now. I'll catch you later."

"Yeah, okay," I said. "Listen, thanks. I mean, really, I owe you one."

He left and I lay there, holding the ice pack to my head and waiting for the pain to subside.

CHAPTER SEVEN

It's bad enough when your head is aching and someone begins pounding on your door, but when it's your
coach it's doubly painful.

I got to my feet, walked over to the locked door,
and let Coach Griffin in. He began to speak as he closed
the door behind him. "Okay, Doyle, why'd you miss
the . . . ?" He stopped short as he got a look at me.

"I was resting," I said.

"Take your hand away from your face." I did. He
drew in a long breath. "Why don't you sit down and tell
me what happened, from the beginning."

I sat down on my bed and he sat down on Shawn's,
facing me. He waited patiently for a minute or two, and
then asked, "Are you in pain?"

"No. Not really."

"Do you need medical care?"

"I don't think so. Just this ice."

"So what happened?"

"It was my own stupidity," I mumbled. "I came back
from practice in a hurry to change, and I walked into the
bathroom door."

Coach Griffin studied me carefully. "You got a black eye by walking into a door?"

"Yes, sir."

"Does this happen to you often?"

"Never happened before." I couldn't tell whether he believed me or not. "I guess I was excited by the press conference and all. Anyway, I didn't want to come down and get my picture taken with all the swelling. . . ."

"I can understand that."

"And it was painful at first. So I thought I'd better just lie down."

"That was probably a good idea, Doyle. Now let me ask you a question. Do you have any respect for me at all?"

"Yes, sir. A lot."

"And yet you tell me a story like that?"

I took the ice pack away from my head and set it down on the floor. It started to make a tiny puddle. "Go put that in the bathroom sink before you stain the wood," he said. "And be careful of the door."

I put the melting ice pack in the sink, returned, and sat back down.

"So?" he said. His voice now had a hard edge.

"Like I told you before, it was just an awkward accident."

"Doyle, I feel sorry for victims, but I don't have much patience with liars. I can send you home this afternoon."

I had been through a lot that day, and my voice suddenly shot way up. "LOOK, WHAT DO YOU WANT

ME TO SAY? IF YOU DON'T BELIEVE ME, THEN
YOU TELL ME WHAT HAPPENED!"

Coach Griffin stayed completely cool. "If I had to
guess, I'd say somebody punched you in the eye. And
you're afraid to tell me who and why because you think
your teammates won't respect you."

"Even if I didn't walk into a door, I walked into a
door."

"What I don't understand," Coach Griffin said with
real bewilderment, "is that you haven't been here long
enough to make anybody want to punch you in the
head."

"That's true."

"And yet you have a black eye."

"Is it real bad?"

"It doesn't look very good." He frowned. "Jimmy,
I'm tempted to send you home on the next plane out,
because things I don't understand make me uncomfortable."

"You're not the only one who feels that way."

He gave me a slightly puzzled look. We weren't quite
connecting in this strange conversation. "And what
don't you understand?"

"Who's Devonne Saunders? Why did he think he
was a starter on this team?"

My question seemed to catch Coach Griffin by surprise. "Where did you hear about that?"

"Like I said, there are things I don't understand."

"Well, Devonne was our mistake," he admitted.
"When you said you didn't want to play on our team,

73

Coach McNeil and I decided to wait a little while in case you changed your mind. Eventually I called your mom and she talked some sense into you, but while that was going on, Coach McNeil and I got our signals crossed. He thought we were done waiting, so he called Devonne and talked to him about your spot. He didn't exactly offer it to him, but when you decided to come, we were in a bind.

"We sat down with Devonne and explained to him what had happened. We had already promised our other nine spots and there was little we could do. We offered to bring him with us to this training camp, in case someone got hurt, and even to Rome as a kind of junior assistant coach. But he had other invitations to play in June, and said no. I guess there were some hard feelings."

"Too bad," I said. "He probably was a better guard than me."

"Have you ever seen him play?"

"No, but that's what everyone else seems to think. Hell, anybody was probably better than me today."

Coach Griffin stood up. "Run on home, then," he said. "You can fly back to Minnesota this evening. I'll get you a ticket any time you say. Or you can come down to practice after lunch. One or the other. You decide. But let me tell you something first. We scouted Devonne and we scouted you, and we invited the best guard we saw. We're strong inside and Augustus can handle the ball, but we needed a long-range shooter, in case we go up against a bigger team with a great zone defense, which in Europe is very likely. You're the best pure shooter we saw. . . ."

"I was good in Granham, Minnesota. I couldn't even get off my shot here."

He shrugged. "All the rest of them have had regional or even national experience. You've just had local. When Chris and I decided to put this team together, we agreed that since it was gonna represent young America, we'd reach out to all parts of the country. We wanted to try to get some talent that might not have been tapped before, away from the big urban centers. Some new faces."

"So you wanted me because I'm white?"

"I won't even dignify that with an answer," Coach Griffin said and walked out of my room.

I got up and paced around. I didn't need this. Back home in Granham I was a basketball hero and things were a lot less complicated. I could be with Janey, and my family, by next morning. I pulled my suitcase out and began packing it, but I had only put in three pairs of socks when I picked it up and hurled it across the room.

I walked out into the sunshine. I didn't need this, I told myself over and over. Maybe I couldn't play at their level, but I also didn't deserve to be humiliated. I walked around in an angry daze — my feet could have led me anywhere on the large campus, but for some reason they took me down the long hill. I didn't need this. I reached the brown-and-white concrete shell of Pauley Pavilion and hesitated for a long time. A voice inside me said, "Stop, go back, you don't need to subject yourself to this. You'll only make a fool of yourself. You don't need this."

But after several minutes in limbo, I entered the gym.

They were running a layup drill at high speed. As I walked closer, I listened to the screech of sneakers on wood, and the *thud, thud, thud* of bouncing basketballs. Heads turned one by one to look at me as I approached. Augustus LeMay met my glance and then went back to the drill.

Coach Griffin whistled for a time-out. "Okay, all of you, get your butts over here," he shouted. "Anybody talks or wises off, they're gonna be running wind sprints till their legs fall off."

There was complete silence.

Coach McNeil walked out and stood next to Coach Griffin as he spoke to us in a serious voice. "One of our best players was hit on the nose with a basketball this morning, shooting around after practice," he said. "It bled all during the press conference. Another one of our best players walked into a bathroom door and got a black eye at just about the same time. Now, normally, if I were coaching a team, I'd say both of those guys are a little too clumsy to play on the international level."

He paused to let his sarcasm hit home. "So I'd send them home, no questions asked. But since we've all just gotten here, I'm going to go against my own best instincts." For a second he looked right at me. "I'm going to give all of you a chance to be less clumsy." His glance swung to Augustus LeMay. "One chance. And that's it. Any questions?"

There were none.

"Okay," he said. "Then let's forget these accidents ever happened and play some hoop!"

CHAPTER EIGHT

Three sunny days rolled by in succession, as things got steadily better for me.

The team practiced for two hours in the mornings, broke for lunch, and hit the court again for three more hours in the afternoons. Then we had time free for swimming, tennis, and sightseeing.

We went to Mann's Chinese Theater in Hollywood and saw the handprints and footprints of past and present screen legends. A tour bus took us around the lavish homes of the great Hollywood stars. I took pictures out the window as our guide told us who lived or used to live in the different mansions. I had never seen such houses — some of them looked larger than Granham High School and it was difficult to believe that only one family lived in each of them.

Our press conference had generated a lot of publicity and we received a number of invitations, including one to a Dodger game. I'm a big baseball fan and I had been to a couple of Twins games back home, so I really enjoyed going to the southern California version of a major league park. There were spectacular palm trees behind the outfield fences, and they sold Mexican food along with hot dogs at the concession stands.

The next afternoon, we got to have our picture taken with the mayor in City Hall, and then toured Olivera Street and Chinatown. Olivera Street has been restored to the way Los Angeles looked a hundred years ago, and there were mariachi bands and booths selling all kinds of Mexican crafts from clothes to jewelry to delicious burritos and tacos.

Chinatown, only a few blocks away, was also exotic, but with a completely different flavor. Many signs were written vertically in Chinese characters, there seemed to be millions of restaurants with strange names like Li Fat and Wong Lo, and in several windows we glimpsed whole barbecued ducks hanging up for sale. The strangest store we came across was an herb shop, with thousands upon thousands of withered and gnarled roots in tiny jars. I guess they're used as medicine, but some of them looked as if they would be pretty difficult to swallow down, no matter what was wrong with you.

I had been a little bit scared of Los Angeles when I first got off the plane, but the city we toured had a pulse and glamor that continually amazed me. Augustus Le-May didn't come on any of our sightseeing trips. I remembered Shawn saying that Augustus had had a hard childhood, and I sort of wondered how hard things could have been for him growing up in this exciting city. Small-town life is fine, but I have to admit L.A. sure seemed a lot more exciting than Granham, Minnesota.

I tried to imagine what it would have been like if I had grown up in a place where the weather was perfect year-round, the sandy beaches stretched for miles, and everyone seemed to have a perfect body, an expensive car, and a fun, laid-back approach to life. It didn't sound too bad. And I tried to imagine Augustus LeMay shoveling snow and playing his star-quality basketball in our little high school gym. It wasn't his style — in fact, there wasn't much style there at all.

Maybe if he tried doing all the lifting and stocking and sorting at a small-town hardware store for hour after hour on weekends, when his friends were out having fun, he'd learn a few things about just how hard and dull childhood can be. There seemed to be endless malls in Los Angeles, and the flashing neon from different movie cineplexes strobed every few blocks as we toured around the city. I wondered how Augustus would cope with living in a town with one main street, one diner that stayed open past ten, and one movie theater that showed mostly family movies.

The houses and apartment buildings we passed as we drove around Los Angeles came in all different shapes and sizes, but they all looked pretty comfortable to me. Could the room Augustus slept in when he was growing up have been any smaller than mine, or looked out on a less interesting view? Could he have walked the exciting streets of Los Angeles with less spare change jingling in his pocket than I'd had back in Granham? I dated a rich girl and had friends whose parents gave them generous allowances for doing nothing at all, while I'd worked hard for every penny since grade school. Could Augustus have seen people with more, or been given less?

As our team explored Los Angeles together, I started to become friends with the other guys. I got to know all of them a little bit, but I spent most of my time hanging out with my roommate Shawn and his two friends, Stinger and Ray. Sometimes Patterson, the other white player on the team, tagged along, but mostly he spent his free time playing video games with a reserve guard named Bell. Anthony Bell was from Philadelphia and he was by far the shyest guy on our team — he had a friendly smile but he said very little.

Shawn was an all-around terrific guy. I couldn't have been luckier with a roommate, and I sometimes wondered whether Coach Griffin and Coach McNeil — perhaps guessing that I would have some difficult adjustments to make — hadn't done me a little favor by putting me with him.

Shawn only seemed to care about three things on this earth, but he liked those three an awful lot. First was basketball — he would stay after practice to shoot around till they turned the lights off in the gym. Second was eating. He could ingest prodigious quantities of just about anything, and a few hours later he'd start asking me if I knew what we were having for our next meal. Lastly, he loved sleeping, and from lights out to morning wake-up call he would lie there with his feet hanging off the end of the bed, snoring happily away with a look of absolute peace and contentment on his babyish face.

The only problem we had as roommates was his snoring, a sound that could be either faint and soothingly melodic or as loud and irritating as a garbage disposal, depending upon his sleeping position. "Just throw a shoe at me if I get too loud," he told me. One night, when it sounded like someone was sawing down an oak tree with a blunt power tool ten feet from me, I was tempted to hurl a sneaker at him. In the end I decided against it. No matter what he had said, it didn't seem like such a good idea to throw a basketball sneaker at a slumbering giant.

Stinger, the starting forward from Detroit, played intense, aggressive basketball, but his real love was rapping. He had an incredible knack for making up lyrics off the top of his head. The guys would give him a subject, and without any hesitation Stinger would come out with a whole rap song, perfectly in rhythm, that contained a lot of clever lines and daring rhymes.

He roomed with Patterson. Patterson was a shy, nervous guy from Long Island who spoke in such a low voice that it almost sounded as if he were whispering a secret to you when he said "Good morning." The two of them seemed well suited as roommates, except for the fact that Stinger constantly complained about Patterson's smelly feet. He bought him foot powder, gave him clean socks, and finally made up a rap song called "The Killer Feet" that he sang with mock seriousness, as if it was about something really dangerous and violent. The song began like this:

> Block to block, across the town
> Didja hear? The word's gone down,
> Lock your door, stay off the street,
> Keep away from the killer feet.
> Stretch socks shrank
> And hi-tops sank
> When they got too close
> To that nasty skank . . .

But of all of my teammates, Ray, our team comedian, was by far the most fun to be around. He was a hilarious guy — he could do imitations of both our coaches, right down to the way they talked and walked and grimaced when one of us missed an easy shot. "Get back in the game, Doyle," he used to shout at me two or three times a day, imitating Coach McNeil. "Get your head out of the snow, Doyle. You're not in Minnesota anymore!"

For some reason Ray seemed to like me, and he used me as a straight man for a lot of his jokes. He was never happy calling me Doyle, and by the end of our second day had christened me "Snowman" because I came from such a cold state. I didn't particularly care for the nickname, but it quickly caught on.

"Hey, Snowman," he said as my shots started to go in during our third day of practice, "looks like you can play this game a little bit, after all. We thought maybe they brought you here from the backwoods to make the rest of us look good."

Coach Griffin worked with me before and after practice sessions to make the adjustment to this level. He had been a pro guard himself, and he assured me over and over that I wasn't slow or bad — just sloppy and out of synch with my more experienced teammates. Bad habits that I had picked up in the old gym in Granham cost me every time in Pauley Pavilion — these nine guys pounced on the slightest error. If I telegraphed a pass, Ray would pick it off. If I tried a shot in traffic, one or even two hands would swat it away. But when I played a careful, controlled game I found that Coach Griffin was right — I could stay with these guys. Soon I was even contributing a little bit.

"Snowman is heating up," Ray warned after I played him tough in a tightly fought scrimmage on our third day. "Doesn't want me to take his job away. Don't melt yourself, Snowman."

On my fourth day in Los Angeles we played a local high school all-star team. The game took place in an old high school gym that reminded me a lot of Granham. The rows of wooden bleachers all around the court made me feel kind of at home. As we shot around to warm up, I began to feel like I might have a good game.

The local all-stars must have read *Sports Illustrated* because when the game started they double-teamed Augustus and also tried to double on Shawn whenever he got the ball down low. That strategy left me wide open on the perimeter. Soon my teammates began kicking the ball out to me and yelling for me to put it up from long range.

I hit one shot. Two. Three. "Snowman, Snowman, go Snowman," Ray shouted from our bench each time I ran past. The local all-stars had their strategy and they stuck to it — no matter what damage I did, they refused to cover me outside. I guess they thought I would soon cool off. I swished home two shots from three-point territory. A jumpshot from the corner. One of my patented NBA-length fall-away jumpers. Suddenly my whole team had picked up Ray's chant. Each time I ran by the bench I heard, "Snowman, Snowman, ice them, baby, go, Snowman!"

By the time I fouled out of the game, in the third quarter, I had twenty-six points. The crowd gave me a nice hand and my teammates on the bench greeted me with high fives. Ray got me in a friendly headlock and messed up my hair. "Snowman, you were a monster out there," he said, grinding his knuckles into my scalp. "Let me touch that head for good luck."

"You're gonna dent my skull," I said, struggling to get free, "and my name's not Snowman."

"Where'd you learn to shoot like that with snow and ice all over the playground, Snowman?"

"I only answer to 'Jim' or 'Doyle.'"

"Thompson, stop horsing around," Coach Griffin shouted. "You're in for Doyle at guard. Get out there!" And then, as Ray peeled off his sweats, Coach Griffin thumped me on the shoulder. "Nice shooting, Snowman. You iced them, baby."

When a coach picks up on a nickname, it sticks to you forever.

I felt good that whole afternoon and evening. My black eye had healed, my shots were falling, and I had made some good friends. The only thing bugging me was that the best player on our team still wasn't talking to me, but I told myself that that was his problem and not mine. As least we weren't trading punches.

That evening, just after dinner, I left the dorm to call Janey. The phones in our rooms weren't connected, so my teammates and I used a pay phone by the tennis courts. I fed a small pile of quarters into the slot and dialed. It was seven in Los Angeles, which meant it would be nine o'clock back in Minnesota. Dr. Sutherland answered on the first ring and seemed glad to hear from me. "How are they treating you in the City of Angels?"

"Pretty well so far."

"My daughter seems to miss you a little bit."

"I miss her, too. Is she there?"

"At the moment she's practically wrestling the phone out of my hand," he said. "Ouch. Here . . ."

"Jimmy?"

Hearing her voice made me smile. "How are you?"

"You haven't called in four days."

"I've been real busy."

"Then I'll call you from now on. What's your number?"

"We don't have phones in our rooms. I'm calling from a pay phone. How are things in Granham?"

"Good, but a little lonely," she said. "There was an article about your team in the paper. Actually, I'm reading a couple of different papers' sports sections in case they mention you. There was a team picture with the article. Some of those guys on your team look pretty big."

"They are."

"I went by your mother's store and showed the article to her. She looked lonely, too. Even your two sisters seem to miss you."

"That's hard to believe," I said, thinking of the two monsters. "How's Mom doing in the store?"

"Things looked very busy. She was running around, helping customers. How're you doing in Los Angeles?"

I knew I was supposed to say that I was lonely, too, but I sort of bypassed it. "I've made some good friends. I'm starting to learn the words to a lot of rap and hip-hop. The guys are all incredible athletes. At first I was worried, but I'm finding out that I can stay with them."

"Well, don't stay with them any longer than you have to. The weather's warm here and I don't have anyone to enjoy it with."

"I'll be back soon."

"I wrote you two letters but I don't have any place to send them."

I laughed. "It sounds like you have too much free time. Spending a summer just moping around the house, watching TV and reading, would drive me crazy. Get a summer job."

"I've been helping out at my mom's office."

"Maybe you need something a little more challenging. I'm running out of quarters. I think I'll have to go in a minute."

"If you were here now, I'd give you a big hug and a kiss," she said.

"I wouldn't mind seeing you, either," I told her.

I heard her swallow, and hesitate. "You haven't met any girls in Los Angeles?"

"Janey, all we do here is play basketball. I'll be home in three weeks."

"I know. It's just that I miss you. Call again, soon."

"I don't know if I can afford to, from Italy."

"Call and just give me a number, and I'll call you back. I love you. 'Bye."

I wanted to tell her I loved her back, but I heard my voice just say " 'bye."

I hung up and took a few steps away, and then became aware that someone was watching me. A tall figure sat on a brick wall, in shadow. There was a lamppost about twenty feet away, and when the figure turned his head, I saw a glint of light from a gold earring. He didn't say anything — he just sat there watching.

My path back to the dorm took me within fifteen feet of him. For some reason, I slowed down as I got close. We could just see each other's features through the gathering darkness. "Snowman," he said, with a faint nod.

It wasn't exactly a greeting, but at least it was recognition. "Augustus," I said back. And then, "Can I talk to you for a minute?"

He didn't say yes, but he didn't say no, either.

So I walked over and sat down next to him on the low brick wall. It was warm and breezy, and a sliver of yellow moon was visible beyond the edge of the dorm's roof. "Nice evening," I said.

"Never saw one that wasn't."

"Only it's strange not to be able to see stars."

"Say what?"

"Back in Granham — that's where I'm from — we can see billions of stars. Here in Los Angeles, if you're lucky, you can just see a few. And some of those turn out to be airplanes."

He didn't reply for such a long time that I thought the conversation was over. I was all set to head back into the dorm when he surprised me by saying, "The stars in this town live in Malibu, and they shine down on Hollywood. Didn't you go on those stupid trips?"

"I didn't think they were so stupid."

"Then you saw the stars of L.A."

I didn't know what to say. "I guess the ones in the sky are hidden by smog."

Augustus had expressed no interest up till then in who I was or where I came from, so I was a little surprised when he asked, "So how many people live in this place . . . Granham?"

"About eight thousand."

"In the whole city?"

"It's a town. Some of those eight thousand live on farms."

"Your family have a farm?"

"No. We run a little hardware store."

He didn't say anything else for a while so we just sat there. Maybe five or ten lights were on in dorm rooms. Some of the guys must have been reading or just lying around. On most evenings, my teammates gathered in the lounge after dinner to watch TV.

"You hit some shots today, Snowman," Augustus finally said.

"They were doubling and tripling on you, so they left me wide open."

"Even so. When I say something that turns out to be wrong, I like to set it straight," he said. "I was wrong about you. You can play."

"I'll never be as good as you."

"No," he agreed, "and you'll never be as good as Devonne, either. But you got a game."

Since he had brought it up, I decided to attack our problems head on. "About Devonne . . . I don't know what you think or what you heard, but I had absolutely nothing to do with his not being invited. Coach McNeil and Coach Griffin flew out to Granham and offered me a place on this team, so I came. That's all I know about it."

"And all I know is that my cousin was invited and then they dropped him to make room for a white boy who isn't as good. And that's why I got angry. It still doesn't seem right."

I didn't want to get into another argument, but I had to ask, "Do you always think of people as black or white?"

"What color are you?"

"White," I answered.

"And what color is Devonne?"

"I guess he's black."

"You're here, going to Italy. He's not. That's what I think."

"We don't have many black people in Granham," I told him.

"It doesn't sound like you got many people there at all, Snowman."

"That's true," I admitted with a smile, "so I don't know much about what goes on in a city like Los Angeles. I'm probably pretty clueless. . . ."

"If you know you're clueless about something, it might be best to talk less."

"But . . . it's unfair to judge me just because I'm white. I had to write a paper in high school on the 'I have a dream' speech, where Martin Luther King said he had a dream that his children would *not* be judged by the color of their skin, but by the content of their character. What's true for Dr. King's children should be true for me, too."

Augustus looked at me, shook his head, and laughed. He was a serious kind of guy, and his laugh caught me completely by surprise. It wasn't a happy laugh — it rang with anger and disbelief. "So that's what you studied in school, about black people, in your town with the farms and the stars in the sky?"

"That's what we studied."

"You never read anything else on the subject?"

"I don't read much in general. But I thought that 'I have a dream' speech was really something."

"Yeah, it was really something," Augustus repeated. Then he looked around at the lighted tennis courts. Behind them it was just possible to make out the outlines of gently swaying trees. "It's nice up here in Westwood," he said. "All that pine almost smells like perfume. And it's safe. Do you hear me, Snowman?"

"I hear, but I don't think I'm understanding."

"And I'm speaking, but I don't think I'm communicating."

"Try again."

"I didn't grow up here," Augustus said. "I grew up in a whole different city — a million miles from here. On the streets where I grew up, we didn't put much faith in dreams. I don't want to take anything away from Dr. King. But his vision doesn't really speak to me. If he had a dream, that means he must've been asleep. He must've been unconscious. I'm wide awake. You understand that?"

"I don't see why that should mean that we can't shake hands or be friends. I grew up poor and I don't blame anybody for it. And I'm sure not asking for any sympathy. The last few days I haven't just been sitting here in Westwood — I've been all around this city, from the homes of the old movie stars to a Dodger game to City Hall to Chinatown, and L.A. looks pretty good to me."

"Sounds like they gave you the grand tour."

"I know there are bad areas, too, but all in all . . ."

"All in all, Snowman, you were right when we started talking. You don't have a clue." He stood up. "And I'm not going to waste my breath."

I held out my right hand. "You seem like a good guy and you're a hell of a basketball player. Will you shake my hand?"

"If you keep holding it out there, your arm might get tired," he told me. "In *The Autobiography of Malcolm X*, a white girl from some college hears Malcolm speak and follows him all the way back to New York. She asks him what she can do to help. And maybe she was sincere in reaching out to him. Maybe she wasn't. But he told her, 'Nothing.' You got that?"

I slowly lowered my hand to my side.

Augustus nodded. "You do your thing, I'll do mine. You played a good game today. You hit your shots. That's all. Good night, Snowman."

"Good night," I said.

CHAPTER NINE

More than half of us had never been to Europe before, so as the day of our departure drew near, excitement built steadily. There were lots of conversations in the TV lounge about what kind of rooms, food, and entertainment we could expect. Different hotels in Rome were sponsoring different teams in the tournament, and we found out that we were going to be staying at a hotel in the center of Rome, off a piazza, or square, called Campo dei Fiori.

"It's one of the very prettiest squares in Rome," Coach McNeil, who had played two years of professional basketball in Italy, told us over dinner. "There's a big iron statue in the center of a man who was burned to death a few hundred years ago for his religious views."

"A statue of some sucker who got torched doesn't sound too cheerful," Ray Thompson observed.

"I admit the statue's a little ominous, but the piazza's a very hip and cheerful place," Coach McNeil assured us. "There's a flower and fresh produce market in the mornings, and young people gather there in the evenings to sip coffee, eat ice cream, and just rub shoulders. You guys are gonna love it."

"So it's close to the action?" Ray wanted to know.

"The only action you're going to be seeing is on the basketball court," Coach McNeil told him. "You're gonna be so tired from games and practices that you're not going to have any energy left over for getting into trouble."

"I just want to experience fun in another culture," Ray said innocently, with a suggestive smile that made us all laugh.

"I'll arrange some fun for you," our coach replied. "Sightseeing tours. History lectures. And how about a trip to the Vatican?"

"That wasn't exactly what I had in mind."

Later, in the TV room, Ray elaborated on what he did have in mind. "I hear the club scene in Europe is wild. They don't close, like in L.A. — some of them go all night. And they don't have a drinking age — the Europeans are cool about that. Best of all, I hear the chicks love Americans and basketball's a hot sport. As athletic stars, we're gonna be fighting them off."

"And what about Coach M and Coach G coming by for bedroom checks every night at ten-thirty?" Shawn asked.

Ray shrugged. "Three weeks in Rome. Plenty of time to throw Coach a few fakes."

I was as excited as Ray was, but not about staying out late and chasing Italian girls. The picture of Janey that I carried around in my wallet sort of killed that impulse. For me it was more about seeing a place outside America for the first time. I had a very personal reason for being curious about Italy. My mother's father had been a fisherman in Bari, and my grandmother had been from Naples. Both of those cities are in the south, and Rome is in the center of Italy, but even so I felt as if I was going to see a part of my family's past.

My bags were both pretty much all packed and ready to go two days before we were set to leave. Besides basketball and hanging with the guys, I spent a lot of time reading. At the campus bookstore I found a copy of *The Autobiography of Malcolm X*, the book that Augustus had referred to in our conversation. Even though I don't usually read very much, I whipped through it in my spare time.

I felt shy about reading it in front of my teammates, so I read it mostly in my room, when Shawn wasn't around. It was very different from any book I had ever read before.

I couldn't help liking Malcolm and eventually even sympathizing with him. When he joined the Nation of Islam and came to believe that "white devils" were to blame for all the misfortunes that he and other black people had suffered, he lost me. My great-grandparents weren't slaveowners, but rather poor Irishmen and even poorer Italians. And my grandparents were penniless immigrants. But at the same time, I understood that Malcolm X was speaking of the harsh and racist world he had lived in since childhood.

I had always known that slavery was an ugly stain on America's history, but I guess I had never really considered what it meant to kidnap people and imprison them for the rest of their lives, just to make money from their labor. Malcolm X saw lots of connections between slavery and the plight of blacks in twentieth-century America.

I was sitting in my room finishing the last chapter, two nights before we were supposed to leave for Italy, when a knock sounded on my door and a voice called, "Hey, Shawn? They're showing the end of the game on ESPN. . . ." Before I could reply, Augustus opened the door.

"He's not here," I said, trying to hide what I was reading.

Augustus nodded, and began to close the door. Then he spotted the book and stopped. "Snowman?"

"What?"

He stepped into the room, and nodded toward the book.

"It bothers me when people don't like me and I can't figure out why," I told him. "I want to at least try to understand."

"Don't waste your time."

"Reading this wasn't a waste of time. But there's one thing I want to ask you."

He waited.

"The other night you told me that story about the girl who heard Malcolm X speak at her college and then followed him to New York and asked how she could help. And he told her that there was nothing she could do."

"It's in there."

"Yeah, that story's in the book, just like you told it to me, but later on Malcolm X says he regretted telling her that."

Augustus stood there, looking down at me. "They shouldn't have even let you buy that book, 'cause you could never in a million years comprehend it," he finally said.

"If I can read it, why can't I comprehend it?"

"You confuse me, Snowman," he muttered, and left the room, closing the door behind him.

The next day was our last in Los Angeles. At the end of our usual morning practice, a few members of the Los Angeles Lakers surprised us by showing up. I had never met pro players before. We got their autographs, and two of them even shot around with us a little bit.

It's inspirational and at the same time frightening to realize how good you can get at something at the very highest level. These professional players were basketball gods. They had such quickness, body control, and touch on their shots that they seemed almost superhuman. At the same time, they couldn't have been more friendly. I even got a little free advice about playmaking in Europe. "The biggest difference is that European basketball goes at a slower, more controlled pace," one of the Laker guards told Augustus and me. "Fast break them every chance you get. Keep forcing the pace and you can run away from them."

After lunch we held our last American press conference. The media came out in force — there must have been five different TV camera crews and twenty print journalists there. We posed for pictures with the pros, and then repeated over and over again in interviews that we didn't think we were favorites and that we'd be happy just to do well.

After a light scrimmage that afternoon, we had a final team meeting before our trip. The assistant coaches passed out luggage tags and reminded us to keep our passports with our carry-on bags. "And we don't want any trouble at all going through customs," Coach Griffin said. "Use your heads. I don't even have to say anything about any kind of drugs, or anything like that. And don't pack anything that resembles a weapon. If you have something that could get you into any kind of trouble — and I know you don't, but just in case any of you do — throw it out here in Los Angeles. Let's show up in Rome with good vibes. Now, we leave for the airport bright and early, so I want all of you in your rooms by ten o'clock tonight."

We had dinner at a steak house in Beverly Hills. My mother wouldn't have approved, but the big slab of prime rib tasted pretty good to me. A little red meat now and then can't be too harmful. Shawn had two prime rib dinners and asked Coach Griffin if he could order a third. "Last taste of American beef for a while," he explained.

"I think two prime ribs are enough," Coach Griffin told him. "We want to make sure our plane can get off the ground."

When we got back to the dorm, I called home and said good-bye to my mother and the two monsters.

Mom had surprising news for me: Janey was helping her out in the hardware store. I figured Janey was probably earning minimum wage — I knew Mom really couldn't afford to pay much more than that, but that Mom's pride probably wouldn't let her accept Janey's help for free. It was a little strange to think of them working together in that little store, flipping through different newspapers' sports sections looking for articles, and no doubt talking about me to each other.

The more I considered it, the more I thought that working in the hardware store might be good for Janey — it would show her what life is like for most people. Sometimes it felt like she almost thought there was something wrong with me for having to work so hard and having so little to show for it. There had been many sunny weekends in Granham when she wanted to hang out together and have fun but I needed to work at the store. And there had been lots of evenings when she wanted to have dinner out or even take a trip to Minneapolis to go to a movie or a concert, and I either had to make excuses or admit that I just couldn't afford it.

I know she tried to avoid making me feel bad, but she didn't always succeed. How could she possibly understand my situation, when she'd never worked an honest day in her life? The only "job" Janey had ever had before this was helping with the paperwork in her mother's medical practice, and that never seemed like real work to me. Her mother paid her six dollars an hour to sit in an air-conditioned office and shuffle papers around. Now, at least, she would get her hands dirty, feel tired at the end of the day, and realize how hard it is to save money when you're working for minimum wage.

Bed check that night was half an hour earlier than usual. Coach Griffin told us that he wanted us all to get a good sleep, because we had a very long day ahead of us. "Night, Snowman," Shawn said, settling happily into his favorite sleeping position. "If I snore, you know what to do."

"Cram a high-top in your mouth?"

"With a little mustard," he said, and was soon sound asleep.

I drifted off a little bit later, and slept soundly. I had a strange dream, about Janey running off with a tribe of Gypsies. In my dream, my mother was the Queen of the Gypsies, and she made Janey tell fortunes to earn her keep. The dream was getting really weird when suddenly I was snapped out of it by a strange sound in my bedroom.

I lay there for a few seconds, still half asleep. Over the lawnmower roar of Shawn's snores, I could distinguish a sharper sound. Tapping. Knuckles on glass. Finally I got out of bed and went to the window. Augustus was standing out there, dressed in dark clothes. A red bandana covered his shaved head. I opened the window.

He slid easily into my bedroom, and threw a glance at Shawn. "How do you sleep through that?"

"I pretend it's a thunderstorm. What's going on?"

"Get dressed."

"We can't go anywhere. Coach Griffin already came by."

"*I said* get dressed. There's no time . . ."

"No time for what? . . . Is somebody in trouble?"

He didn't answer, but I felt a strange sense of urgency. After looking at him for a few seconds, I began pulling on some clothes. Sweatpants. A black T-shirt. Sneakers. When I was dressed, he slipped back out and I followed him, pushing the window carefully shut behind us. We tiptoed through the shrubbery, past other dorm rooms, and then sprinted away into the darkness.

CHAPTER TEN

A gray van was waiting on Gayley Avenue, just off the grounds of the campus. It looked ominous sitting there on the quiet street, with its motor idling and its lights off. Two guys got out of the van. The driver looked a little older than Augustus and me. He had the sculpted bulk of a bodybuilder — when he moved, muscles rippled on his remarkably broad shoulders and massive arms. I didn't get a clear look at the third guy, who was wearing a crimson cap pulled low over his forehead. Instinctively I slowed down. "What's going on?" I asked Augustus. "Who's in trouble?"

"You are," he said. And at that moment, strong hands grabbed me and I found myself being half dragged and half carried toward the van. I started to struggle but they were very strong and had taken me by surprise. Almost before I knew what was happening, I was inside the gray van, the door slid shut, and we started to roll away, down the block.

The bodybuilder had ended up back in the driver's seat, and he was guiding the van through the darkness quickly and skillfully. For a few seconds I was paralyzed with surprise and fear. I took short quick breaths and tried to figure out what to do next. "Whatever you guys are doing, this is a big mistake," I finally said.

"You hear that, G?" Augustus said. "Snowman's going to report us to the police."

The big guy inspected me in the rearview mirror with a quick glance. "That right?"

"If you just bring me back and let me go, I'll never tell anybody about this. None of us want trouble."

As if to prove me wrong, the guy in the passenger side of the front seat looked right at me and pulled off his crimson cap. He was almost a carbon copy of Augustus, except that he was maybe three inches shorter. He had the same handsome features, the same sleek build that suggested power and speed, and he wore a gold earring.

I looked from him to Augustus and then back to him again. "You're Devonne Saunders," I guessed. He didn't deny it. "Listen," I said, "I heard a little bit about what happened, as far as you being invited to be part of the team and then later told not to come. I really had nothing to do with it."

"Sure," he said. "And I had nothing to do with this."

The gray van plowed eastward through the darkness. All sorts of crazy questions ran through my mind. Why were they doing this to me? Maybe they were going to make me disappear for a few days so Devonne could go to Italy after all. Maybe even they didn't know why they were doing this.

We were on Sunset Boulevard, taking the curves of

the winding slope so fast that I had to grab onto the iron frame of my seat so as not to slide off. We turned off the boulevard onto side streets. I didn't know my way around Los Angeles, and soon I was completely disoriented. "Where are we going?" I asked.

They ignored me. I held onto the steel frame of my seat and let the gray van carry us quickly through the darkness. The van didn't have a built-in sound system, but there was a portable player on the floor between the driver and Devonne. Devonne popped a disc in, and rap music began thumping through the car.

The words were fast and rhyming and rhythmic, satiric and sarcastic and angry. The driver, Devonne, and Augustus moved their heads and hands in time to the music. Sometimes Devonne rapped along with the singer.

"You know this, Snowman?" the driver asked.

"Some kind of rap?"

"Gangsta rap," Devonne told me, turning up the volume.

"They don't play too much gangsta rap back home in my part of Minnesota," I told him. "Where are we going?"

"What've you seen so far in L.A.?" the driver asked. He had a booming voice and could project it clearly over the music.

I had almost to shout to make myself heard. "All over. Beverly Hills. Westwood. Santa Monica. Hollywood. And we went to a Dodger game."

"All over," Augustus echoed my words, and they had a good laugh.

"Yeah, well, we're gonna show you around just a little bit more," the driver told me. "They took you on their tour of L.A., and now we're going to take you on ours. We'll visit a couple of hot spots they seem to have missed in the air-conditioned buses."

"Why are you guys doing this to me?"

"To complete your education," Augustus LeMay said, and the other guys laughed.

We drove without talking for fifteen or twenty minutes. Highway gave way to highway as we sped along at seventy miles per hour. "Those are the Mexican ghettos," the driver finally said, pointing to row upon row of small wooden houses built very close together on hillsides. The strange thing was that in his own way, our tough driver did sound like a sort of tour guide. "All gang controlled. Mexican gangs are different from black gangs. They're more like the Mafia — family, family, family. If your father's in, and your brother, then you're in, too. They take kids when they're seven or eight. Teach them the tricks, where to go, who to hang with."

"Yeah," Augustus said, in time to the rap music. "You tell him."

"That's right. Tell him, G," Devonne seconded.

With the beat of the music pounding away in the background, the driver's explanations sounded like an angry rap song without rhymes.

"You got the P-13's, the 18th Street East, West,

North, and South — they don't like blacks too much. We get out of this car right here and inside of five minutes we got guns to our heads."

"Then let's not get out," I suggested.

We drove for a few more minutes at high speed and then turned off the highway and descended a ramp into a long and empty urban street. "Welcome to South Central," the driver told me.

"This is where we passed our tender childhoods," Devonne said.

"Till my aunt moved us out," Augustus added. "Didn't want the 'hood to take us under. That's what we call it. We say, 'You hear about Augie? Tough luck. The 'hood took him under.'"

The driver slowed as we passed a grim three-story building with iron bars almost completely hiding the few windows and thick chains over the doors. "That's not a prison," the driver told me, pointing to the concrete walls and bars and chains. "That's our junior high school."

In my mind's eye, I compared it to Granham Junior High back home. When I hadn't been able to concentrate on math or science, I had always looked out large windows at green fields or a snow-white landscape that rolled away into the distance.

"You know the first thing you learn there?" the driver asked. "You take one look at that place and if you got any brains in your head, you say 'Society's not gonna protect me. They put some bars up on the windows, but those bars're not gonna keep out nothing. So I better protect myself.' How're you gonna do that?"

"I don't know," I said. "Lay low?"

"You lay low, you stay low," the driver said. "You start hanging with a gang, you get a name, you get respect on the street — that's how you protect yourself."

Devonne cut in. "We can send armies to fight Desert Storm, we can send billions of dollars to Russia, so how come we send American kids to a school that looks like that? No windows, metal detector at the door, bullets coming in from the street."

We had left the school behind, and were on a street with two-story development projects. "Those look okay from the outside," the driver said. "Inside, they're murder incorporated. Most times the cops won't even go in after dark. If someone gets iced, they say, 'Bring the body out to us.' "

A car honked and somebody shouted something. Augustus shouted back and made a sign with his hand. "That's a 'B' for 'Blood,' " he said, showing me how he folded his fingers to simulate a "B" shape. "Here's a 'C' for 'Crips.' You hangin' in the wrong turf, you flip the wrong sign, you get a gun to your head."

"Now, that's the 'Alley of Death,' as we call it," the driver cut in, pointing to a dark and narrow alley between two brick buildings. "I got two friends who were killed in that alley. Nice guys, but the 'hood took them under. And here's a street I want to show you. This is Boyle Street."

It was a wide, long, and open street. The few buildings were set way back from the curb. There were weed-choked lots and burnt-out streetlights. "Notice anything special about Boyle Street?"

"It's wide open." I hesitated. "I mean, it's got a good view."

"Hey, Snowman's got some smarts," Devonne said.

"You called it, baby," the driver told me. "You can see for miles. So this is where they take a kid to jump him into a gang."

"What's that?"

"Oh, man, you don't get into a gang right away. First you hang. Learn the streets. They put a deuce-deuce — a twenty-two — in your hands and let you shoot it. See how you like the feel. When they think you're ready, they jump you in. Six, maybe seven members take you out here to Boyle. And they beat on you. Face. Pow. Ribs. Pow. You go down, they wait for you to get back up. They want to know how long you'll fight back. Maybe after a few punches and kicks you just cover up and beg. Then you're not strong enough to be in their gang. So they jump you in to see if you fight back."

"I can see that life is tough here," I said to Augustus as we drove away from Boyle Street. "What I can't understand is why you hate white people. All the violence you're telling me about seems to be gang on gang."

"Look around, Snowman," Devonne demanded angrily. "My aunt can earn four twenty-five an hour at Mickey D's. Is that gonna feed her family of six? You see stores here?"

"No," I admitted. "Where do people shop?"

"The Slauson Swap Meet for clothes. One or two lousy grocery stores dare to open their doors to sell food. You think a bank's gonna give me a loan to start a new business? All we got is liquor stores and churches on every corner, and both of them keep us down. You saw our school. We got no safe parks. No rec halls. In jail at least they have beds and hot food. What real choice does the system white people built give us, man? You say gang on gang? Black on black? You blame us? I blame you."

I watched South Central Los Angeles glide by the van's window. We rattled over some railway tracks and our driver slowed down and let the van's headlights play on a wall filled with colorful, striking images. "That's graffiti," he said. "Street art. Should be hanging in a museum instead of stupid framed pictures of apples and oranges." He pointed to a nearby wall that was covered with crude writing and gang slogans. "That's tagging. Not art at all. Just pollution."

Part of me wanted to argue with them further, and part of me just wanted to keep my mouth shut and take it all in. Augustus was watching me keenly, and I guess he could see some of what was running through my mind. "Go ahead and say it," he prompted.

"Okay. Sure, it's tough here, but you guys give yourselves a lot of sympathy. My grandparents came here with nothing. Broke Italians and dirt-poor Irish. They worked and saved and struggled to make their own breaks. My parents took up their struggle and carried it to the next step by opening a little hardware store. It's not much, but it's a lot more than my grandparents had. That's the American way. Slowly, through hard work, you pull yourself up."

"Your grandparents came because they wanted to come," Augustus answered. "My ancestors were brought over like cattle. Somebody said, 'There are big, tall, strong men in Africa. Let's get them to do our work for us.' Your grandparents may have been poor, but they brought their culture, their religion, their family, their pride, and their identity with them. Mine were stripped of everything. Manhood. Language. Customs. They took away our drums. Took away our spirituality. Raped our women. Took away our belief that we even had a right to think for ourselves and act for ourselves. You don't see a difference?"

"I see a difference."

Our driver turned the van onto a wide street. The boulevard was awash in bright lights and seemed almost to vibrate with car horns and exchanges of loud greetings back and forth from car to car and curb to curb. "This is Crenshaw, a hot spot they seem to have missed on your bus tour," he announced. "But we wouldn't want you to miss it. 'Cause this is the center of the action."

"Yeah, check it out," Devonne half shouted, to be heard above the din of horns.

"Look close, but don't stare at anyone, Snowman," Augustus chimed in. "You're just passing through on the midnight tour."

Cars that had been jacked way up on "fixed" suspensions went by bumping up and down, while music pounded from dozens of radios. "You got the car clubs, the Sixty-fours, the Impalas," our driver explained. "There's parking on the islands and a couple of stores, and it's safe to hang here. Everyone leaves it alone."

We cruised on down Crenshaw, and Augustus, Devonne, and particularly our driver exchanged greetings with a dozen or so people we passed. "You seem to know half the people in this city," I said.

"G here knows the streets," Augustus told me. "He's got a name and they give him his respect."

"Are you in a gang?" I asked. "Is that what 'G' stands for?"

"You don't want to be asking people here if they're in gangs," Devonne advised me.

"I don't mind talking to Snowman," our driver said. "Who's he gonna tell?" When we stopped for a red light he pivoted around in his seat and glanced at me. "I just got out a month ago."

"Out of a gang?"

"Out of Folsom."

"Is that a college?"

"It's a prison," Devonne said.

"I graduated from the black college of hard knocks," G said, and then he drove on in silence. "Enough bright lights," G finally grunted. "Let's go see the end of the 'hood fairy tale."

We headed away from Crenshaw, and the lights and liveliness quickly gave way to the narrowest, darkest streets we had driven through so far. Every so often we'd pass a group of young men and women, hanging out on a corner. They'd stop whatever they were doing to give our van a long look as we rolled by. "'Hood grasping," G told me. "Protecting their own turf, 'cause nobody else will."

We rolled uphill, and then up a ramp, to an iron gate. The van's headlights illuminated gravestones. In the pitch darkness, they appeared as stark and pale as so many bones scattered haphazardly over rocky turf. G shut off the engine. "Last stop in the tour," he said. "Everybody out."

I felt a little nervous leaving the van. It had seemed a sanctuary of safety throughout the long trip. G and De-vonne soon wandered off. Augustus and I hung by the van, alone. "This is something I never would have seen in my life," I said to him.

Augustus grabbed the iron bars of the graveyard fence, and peered in. "Come with me, Snowman," he said. He hoisted himself up over the fence, slipped between the spikes, and jumped down onto the ground inside. I followed him up, and caught my pants leg for just a second at the top. It ripped free as I launched myself and flew though the air, and then we were side by side facing rows of graves.

The graveyard was built on a little hill, so that it was possible to see the scattered lights and dark patches of South Central in all directions. We stood there for a few seconds in silence, looking out through the fence at the city. Crenshaw Boulevard curled and uncurled like a giant glowworm a few miles away. Without a word,

Augustus led me quickly through the rows of stones. Even in pitch darkness, he seemed to know his way.

"One more year and I'll be leaving the 'hood behind," he said as we slowed down, apparently nearing our destination. "College. The pros. Devonne'll be right with me. He's got a pro game. It's better than yours, Snowman."

"Maybe it is."

"G won't be getting out," Augustus said in the same emotionless low voice. "The 'hood'll take him under." He stopped at a small plot near a leafless tree. "That's my brother," he said, pointing to a small stone. "And that's my old man."

The second of these stones read *William LeMay, Beloved Husband and Father, Rest in Peace.*

"What happened to him?"

Augustus lifted his gaze from the small stone and looked me in the eyes. His strong features were like chiseled marble, and his intense eyes caught the spectral glow of the half moon. "He was shot running from a cop. Cop told him to stop. Three times. Stop. Stop. Last chance. Stop. Then he shot my old man in the back. A young white cop. Twenty-four years old. Said he was just aiming for the legs."

"Why didn't your father stop running?"

"He worked on a road repair crew and the drilling had made him deaf as a bat," Augustus answered very softly. "He was running to meet me. I was twelve and I'd gotten into some trouble and he was coming full speed to help." He shrugged his muscular shoulders.

"I heard the shot and wondered what had happened. Found him in a pool of his own blood. He died in my arms. With that white cop holding his gun on both of us."

"I'm sorry," I said. "I was with my father when he was dying, too. It's a terrible thing. They even had the same first name . . ."

"You don't know anything about my old man, and I don't know anything about yours," Augustus whispered in an angry hiss. "We're from two different worlds." He seemed furious that I was trying to draw some kind of connection between us and what had happened to our fathers. "Don't go calling me friend and brother, and telling me what all we have in common."

Then Augustus turned and started walking away from his father's grave. I let him get ten or fifteen feet away before I followed him back toward the van.

CHAPTER ELEVEN

Half an hour later and just twenty miles northwest, the gray van climbed past million-dollar homes. Once again the lights of L.A. glittered beneath us, but the view of the city seemed different from this vantage point. No rap music blared. There was no conversation inside the van. The visit to the graveyard had left us all subdued and drained.

G seemed to know this neighborhood just as well as he knew his way around Boyle Street and the "Alley of Death." The van's headlights illuminated Tudor castles and graceful haciendas, mock Italian villas and exotic Far Eastern mansions with pagoda towers. As we climbed still higher the magnificent houses became larger and even more ornate, and hedges and gates screened them from our view.

At last, we reached the end of the cul-de-sac. In front of us, a vast, unfinished structure rambled over an entire hillside. Even in the darkness, I could tell that it was a mansion of monumental proportions. On the grounds I could make out the partially dug pits for two swimming pools, a wooden bridge over a streambed, a tennis court with bleachers, and a little playground with swings, a seesaw, and a jungle gym.

"One of the richest men in Hollywood is building this for his family," G explained. "I hear it'll have more than a hundred rooms. He's been building it for years and years. More than twenty bedrooms. Marble bathrooms. Three elevators. An earthquake-proof security shelter on every floor. I hear there's even a room for sorting and cutting flowers from the garden."

"That's for just one family?" I asked him.

"And their servants," he nodded. "And maybe their servants have servants."

"See, Snowman," Augustus said, "you talked about Martin Luther King and his 'I have a dream.' But how can you have a dream when you can drive through the 'hood and a few miles away someone can build something like this for just his own family?"

I tried to argue. "But Dr. King said . . ."

"None of us want to knock Dr. King," Devonne told me, "but he did things the white man's way. We don't want to overcome *someday*. We want what we want *now*. Malcolm X got it right, an eye for an eye, a tooth for a tooth. If we're pushed, we push back. If I'm kicked, I kick back harder."

"Yeah," Augustus said.

"That's right," G chimed in.

And then everyone fell silent as the red, blue, and yellow lights of a police car suddenly played around us. "Came up the hill with his beams off," G said. "Security guard must've seen us sitting here and tipped him."

The police car rolled to a stop twenty feet from us. Loud amplified instructions boomed out through the night air. "DRIVER GET OUT FIRST. WITH YOUR HANDS IN THE AIR." G obeyed mechanically, as if this was a routine he had gone through before. In fact, all three of them seemed surprisingly calm. I, on the other hand, felt a knot of tension and fear that twisted deep down at the pit of my stomach.

"UP AGAINST THE VAN. HANDS FLAT." G faced us through the window, expressionless, as he pressed his palms on the side of the van. A policeman came up slowly behind him. Another policeman, with a gun trained on him, stood back by the police car, half in shadow.

G was frisked and then questioned. They kept asking him what he was doing there, and he kept repeating that he was just driving around. They wanted to know why he had stopped outside this gate. Was the van his? When G finally was allowed to reenter the van to get registration papers, the cop walked back with him and shined his light into the window.

Our eyes met. He looked very surprised to see me. Then his gaze moved on to Augustus and Devonne. I saw him take a good, careful look at their red bandanas and dark sweats. Then he stepped away from the van with G again.

"This registration expired a month ago," I heard him say. "Anyway, it's not registered to you."

"I borrowed it from a friend," G said. "I'll give you his name and number. Call him up."

"I don't think so," the cop said. "All of you, outside. Hands in the air. Put them against the side of the van." I followed Augustus out of the van, and obeyed the orders. I had never been frisked before and I didn't particularly like it, but the knowledge that the other policeman had a gun trained on us made me follow all the instructions without protesting or talking back.

"Turn around," the cop said when he was done frisking me. I did so, and we looked at each other. He was white, in his late thirties, with a no-nonsense face. "What's the story here?"

There was a long moment of silence, when I hesitated. "We just went out for a drive together," I finally told him. "We haven't done anything wrong."

He looked back at his partner and made a decision. "Something doesn't feel right," he said. "I'm taking all of you in."

Less than an hour later I sat in a small, bare, white-painted room in a police station, denying over and over again that I had done anything wrong. I didn't really want to tell them who I was or why I was in Los Angeles, because I was afraid they would call our coaches and we would get into trouble. But when they asked me my last name and where my parents lived, I had to tell them. That led to other questions about why I was in Los Angeles, who I was staying with here, and how I had found my way into that gray van.

About an hour later, Coach Griffin escorted Augustus, Devonne, and me out of the police station to his shiny BMW convertible. His pencil-thin mustache trembled as his upper lip quivered with anger. He didn't ask for an explanation and we didn't give him one as he drove Devonne home first and dropped him off. Then he drove us back to UCLA. When we reached the campus, instead of turning into the Sunset Canyon dorm lot, he cruised on by and parked near Pauley Pavilion.

"Who knows that you two left your rooms?"

"No one," I said. "My roommate's asleep."

"Mine too," Augustus told him.

He pulled out a key and soon the three of us were standing on the hardwood floor, alone in the vast and empty arena. Coach Griffin had switched on just a very few lights, so the upper rows of bleachers disappeared into ghostly shadows. "Now," he said. "I want to know what's going on with you two."

Augustus and I exchanged a quick look.

"What do you mean?" Augustus asked him.

I had never seen anyone control his anger so well. Coach Griffin's voice never rose even though I could tell his temper was near the snapping point. "I'll tell you exactly what I mean. Almost the first second you two met, you got into a fistfight. Now, the night before we're supposed to leave on an international flight, you break curfew together. The cops catch you trespassing in Bel Air. Wearing gang colors. In the presence of a paroled felon, driving what may be a stolen vehicle. They wake me up at one in the morning to find out if you're really basketball players representing the United

States of America. So let me ask you what they asked me: What the hell is going on?"

Neither of us answered right away. I thought of telling him that my girlfriend back home in Minnesota had predicted that this would be a rough trip, but Coach Griffin didn't strike me as a believer in fortune-telling. "Augustus thought I didn't see the real L.A.," I finally mumbled.

"What real L.A.?"

"He wanted to show me some parts of this city that we haven't visited on team trips. Like South Central . . ."

"You took him to South Central?" Coach Griffin asked Augustus in disbelief.

"Why not? It's part of the city . . ."

"You damn well know why not."

"I brought him back safe," Augustus told him. "We didn't know about any stolen vehicle and we weren't trespassing. If some night watchman hadn't called the cops, we would've been back in the dorms and asleep by now."

"That's not the point," Coach Griffin said.

"So what is the point?" Augustus managed to ask this in a soft voice, without sounding like he was wising off. Instead, he was just cutting to the heart of the matter. "Are you gonna kick us off the team?"

There was a long and silent moment in the vast gym. Coach Griffin looked at both of us. "No," he said. "No, I'm not going to kick you off. But it's good that you're both suited up in sweats and sneakers."

I didn't like the sound of that, and Augustus didn't appear to, either. "Why don't the two of you stretch out for a minute and then get on the end line," Coach Griffin suggested. "Since you have so much energy that you're sneaking out at night and getting into trouble with the cops, we better run a few wind sprints so that you can sleep on the plane." He glanced at his watch. "We have about four hours till daylight."

CHAPTER TWELVE

It's not much fun being stiff and sore on a long plane flight.

Coach Griffin didn't kick us off the team, but he did do a pretty thorough job of kicking our butts with four hours of wind sprints, push-ups, sit-ups, leg lifts, and as many other torturous calisthenics as he could remember from his long playing and coaching career or devise on the spur of the moment.

Augustus was sitting in the aisle seat across from me, and one look told me he was as sore as I was. Some of our teammates seemed to know that something had happened during the night, but they weren't sure exactly what. My calves hurt. My thighs ached. Even my rear end was sore, which didn't make it so terrific to be strapped into an uncomfortable seat. Augustus and I were lucky that we would have a few days to recover when we reached Italy, before our first tournament game. As the big 747 jet rolled down the LAX airport tarmac and took to the skies, I sat back, shut my eyes, and tried to rest.

I was very tired, but for a long time the best I could manage was a strange sort of half sleep. Scenes from the previous night's wild drive through South Central Los Angeles recurred to me in a hazy mixture of sounds and images. Just beneath the roar of the jet engines I heard the shouts and honking horns of Crenshaw Boulevard. When I opened my heavy eyelids a tiny bit to peer out at the thick cloud cover, I glimpsed the bone-white graves of the hilltop cemetery flickering between folds of cumulus mist.

Somewhere in those folds of cloud I nodded off. Hours later and thousands of miles east, the plane bumped down with a jolt and I opened my eyes and asked, "Are we in Italy already?"

"JFK," Shawn told me with a grin. "Go back to sleep. Whatever happened to you last night, you're really out of it today."

I had never been to New York and would have loved to spend a little time seeing the Big Apple, but we never made it out of the airport. Soon we were zooming down the runway again, on our way to retrace the voyage of Columbus in a mere nine hours. As we took off, I pressed my face close to the little window and watched the low-lying airport buildings give way to coastline, and the coastline recede into the horizon as we headed east over the great blue sweep of the Atlantic.

Announcements crackled over the plane's intercom in both flat English and musical Italian. *Slacciare le cinture di sicurezza.* We could undo our seat belts and walk around the cabin. Flight time would be nine hours. *Nove ore.* It was exciting to hear instructions given in a foreign language — it drove home the fact that we were really and truly on our way to Europe.

A very mediocre dinner was served. Ray Thompson, who by now had mock press conferences down to a laughable science, did a takeoff on the chicken ravioli they served us along with cold dinner salad and a roll. He picked up a piece of soggy ravioli and held it on the edge of his fork so that a few bits of chicken were visible. "This is what giving your all for the team is all about," he said as if speaking to a bank of TV cameras. "Some stringy chicken gave one hundred and ten percent of its flesh and blood for this!"

After dinner there was a movie. I bought earphones, but I couldn't hear very well, and I had to keep peering around the head of Jorge Gonzalez. It's a drag when you're trying to follow an action movie and a six-foot seven-inch shot blocker has the seat in front of you. After a few minutes I gave up.

I had been lucky to sleep on the first leg of our flight, but as we crossed the wide Atlantic I stayed painfully awake. Every twenty minutes or so I tried shifting position: legs together under the seat in front of me, legs folded up so that my knees touched the tray table, body turned sideways with my nose pressed into the seat cushion, and arms crossed over my chest.

As I twisted and turned, impressive snores began issuing from the seat next to me. Shawn had fallen asleep sitting straight up, hands on knees and chin tilted way back so that his throat pointed up at the plane's ceiling.

He appeared blissfully out of it, like a giant bear in hibernation, all set to sleep for weeks on end.

ZZZZhhhhhhhh. ZZZZZhhhhhh.

I thought of getting an oxygen mask out of the ceiling compartment and putting it over his mouth, but even a mask probably wouldn't stop the throaty roars. He sounded a little bit like the key-grinding machine in our hardware store back home.

ZZZZZZhhhhhh.

I tried to distance myself from the uncomfortable seat and irritating sounds by thinking about the store, and about Mom and Janey. Maybe Janey would keep working part time when I returned. She probably wasn't getting much for a salary, but then she didn't really need much — her parents gave her more allowance than she could spend. If she helped out and I worked full time, it might even be possible for my mother to take a day off now and then.

I couldn't remember the last time Mom had taken a day all to herself.

The last couple of months she had looked even more tired than usual when she came home after ten or eleven hours at the store. When she walked into our apartment and sat down at her rocker, moving slowly and stiffly, her eyes red with weariness, it made me feel very guilty. Now, on the way to Rome to play basketball, I couldn't help thinking that my mother was the one who really deserved a vacation.

She had never been out of the United States in her life. She hadn't even had a real honeymoon.

My dad had promised to take her to Europe as soon as he could afford it, but the money situation never improved, she got pregnant with me, and they never made the trip. As I sat there, contorting myself into strange positions in the plane's seat, I found myself wondering what life would have been like for Mom and the rest of us if my father hadn't died so young.

Thirty-nine. It seemed as if he had only lived half a lifetime. Maybe even a little less than that — the last six months of my father's life he had been paralyzed by fear.

The interior of the big 747 was dark now, and there were sounds of people sleeping all around me. Blue woolen blankets had been distributed, and people were curled up awkwardly beneath them. Augustus had dozed off in the aisle seat across from me. His shaved head was propped up on a tiny pillow that hid his earring. He even slept gracefully.

The glimpse he had given me into the dangerous streets of his childhood had been scary and the story of how his father had been shot was tragic, but in some ways he had been lucky. His father had gotten it cleanly — one slug through the back. Augustus hadn't seen terror in his father's eyes, or watched a grown man whom he loved break down week by week at the approach of endless darkness. Of all the human fears, I think fear of the grave must be the worst and the most humbling. It digs away at the very roots of what makes a man a man.

We flew into dawn. A wake-up message crackled

over the loudspeaker in Italian and English. We were nearing Leonardo da Vinci Airport. Overhead lights blinked on. Coffee and rolls were served, and Shawn woke up just in time to rub his eyes and help himself to three rolls.

The long night was over. A gentle light spread itself over this foreign land of low hills that looked strangely soft in the first light.

I looked out the window and watched us circle lower and lower over grassy fields, till the runways became visible. And then we were on the ground, and everyone in the plane cheered. "Welcome to Italy," the captain told us over the loudspeaker. "We hope you enjoy your stay. And we'd like to wish good luck to the American Youth Basketball Team. *In bocca al lupo!*"

CHAPTER THIRTEEN

A swarm of two dozen photographers and reporters was waiting for us when we came out of Italian customs. One of them spotted us as we walked through the exit gate and they all came running, pushing past people who were waiting to meet passengers.

It quickly turned into a mob scene. Some of the waiting people shoved the reporters back. Grunts and what I guessed were curses in Italian were exchanged. Flashes from cameras made me blink. A woman screamed as a fistfight broke out between two reporters and a stocky man whom they had bumped with their TV camera. Microphones were thrust into our faces. Questions were shouted at us in English and Italian.

I heard Coach Griffin shouting, "Keep walking for the doors, guys. There'll be a bus. . . ."

Our team's arrival must have gotten some advance publicity in Rome, because fifty or so fans had come to greet us and get our autographs. "Teen Dream Team, Teen Dream Team USA!" they chanted. There were Americans and Italians, old people and young children, and a sizeable number of cute female fans in miniskirts who flashed us welcoming smiles.

"USA! TEEN DREAM TEAM! USA!"

Ray Thompson happened to be standing next to me. "Check this action out," he said with enthusiasm. "I like it here already, Snowman."

A beautiful young woman broke through the line of newsmen and handed me a pen and a pad. "Please, sign," she said in accented English. *"Per favore."* I signed my name and gave the pad to Ray, who flashed the pretty *signorina* a big smile and signed his name. I happened to glance at the pad as he passed it back, and saw that he had written down the name of our hotel. *"Mille grazie,"* she said, and surprised us by stepping forward and kissing us. Ray got the first big smooch and I got the second one, as camera flashes exploded all around us.

"Teen Dream Team! USA!" The mob swept us up and carried us toward the door of the terminal. We became separated and found our way back together — it was a total mess. I heard snippets of interviews in the midst of the chaos. Shawn told a reporter, "I don't know how I like Italy yet. I'm not even out of the airport."

Augustus fought his way through a tight knot of a half-dozen photographers and sportswriters who had surrounded him. I guess news about a team star travels fast, even across the Atlantic. "We're really excited to be here," I heard him say. "And now we need to go to our hotel. Excuse me."

We finally made it outside. Coach McNeil did a quick head check, luggage was stowed in a compartment down below, and our bus began to move forward.

The crowd of reporters and fans followed us a hundred yards or so down the road, snapping pictures and waving. Then they fell back, and we were alone as a team again, cruising through the Italian countryside.

High fives were exchanged. Excited chatter and spontaneous laughter broke out. "It's crazy! We're already superstars in this country!" Jorge Gonzalez said.

"Hey, we're the mean, lean, and very cool Teen Dream Team!" Ray agreed.

Stinger made up a little rap verse on the spot:

> The jet came down on I-talian soil
> A crowd was out, babes and reporters
> Began to boil
> And say, "Hey Dream Team,
> Lean, mean, Dream Team,
> Welcome to Rome,
> Your crazy new home."

I know this sounds strange, but the fields we were driving past had a different look and smell than any farmland I had ever encountered in Minnesota. The countryside itself seemed somehow older, as if thousands of years of human habitation had given the soil and rocks around Rome a special depth of character. It was amazing to think of Roman chariots speeding in the same direction our bus was now traveling, toward the city of Julius Caesar.

My first impression of the city itself was of heavy traffic that flowed back and forth across wide boulevards in random fits and starts. No one seemed to follow any driving rules. Lanes were nonexistent. People halted at some red lights and just drove right through other ones, leaning on their horns. Our bus driver seemed to avoid three accidents by mere inches as he fought his way through nightmare intersections, refusing to yield so much as an inch and shouting out his window at other vehicles.

Every now and then we passed ancient ruins lying right by the side of the road. Once again I was struck by the sheer age of Rome — by the fact that people had prayed at these partially fallen temples and walked among these marble columns more than two thousand years ago. Suddenly Stinger, who was well known for his coolness, shouted, "Whoa! Get a load of that!"

The bus finished turning a corner, and we saw the wreck of the Colosseum barely a hundred yards away. I had seen pictures of the old Roman Colosseum, of course — the place where gladiators fought to the death with swords and tridents, Christians were fed to lions, and emperors gave the thumbs-up or thumbs-down on people's lives. But I had never imagined it was so large and well preserved. Everyone ran to the side of the bus and stared at it as we drove by.

"Would you guys like to come back for a closer look when we get a free day?" Coach Griffin asked.

There was a chorus of yesses.

We finally made it to Campo dei Fiori. It was a gorgeous piazza, with colorful shops all around the perimeter, and a bustling flower and vegetable market going on beneath the iron statue of the man who had been burned to death. Our hotel was in a corner of the square, and the hotel owner himself came out to greet us and show us up to our rooms.

He was a big, good-natured man with an impressive mustache. "Welcome to Rome. I am Ernesto," he announced to us in good English. "A big basketball fan. I like the Chicago Bulls! I like the New York Knicks! While you are here, you are my guests. Anything you want, you come to me."

Shawn and I were roommates again, but the room we were shown to had little in common with the standard dormitory-style room we had shared in the Sunset Canyon complex at UCLA. The tiled ceiling of our room in Rome was fifteen feet high and the dark curtains and wooden fixtures made it feel like living inside one big and expensive antique.

Shawn opened the curtains and we saw a lovely view of the square below. From this high vantage point the flowers turned the market stalls into one enormous garden, while the crowds of shoppers moving back and forth between the old stone buildings formed a colorful and ever-changing background to the bright blooms.

"Hey, Snowman, this is all right!" Shawn said.

I stood behind him, looking down at the magnificent view of our own personal piazza. "Yeah," I agreed. "We're a long way from Granham, Minnesota, but I guess I'm glad I made the trip."

CHAPTER FOURTEEN

We were a little tight before our first game. The expectations for our performance were extraordinary. The past three days had whirled by in a blur of long practice sessions broken up by press conferences and photo ops. The mayor of Rome himself had invited us to his magnificent office to shake our hands and wish us *buona fortuna.*

All tournament games were played in a big new arena where the Roman basketball team played its home games. It looked as if it seated at least thirty thousand, and perhaps half that many people had come to see the Teen Dream Team try to send the Swedish seventeen-and-under squad back to Stockholm.

"Just play your game," Coach McNeil told us. "Don't get psyched. Don't feel you have anything to prove. Don't start hotdogging. Just let it flow."

But of course we all felt we did have something to prove. The other tournament favorites — Spain, Italy, Germany, and Croatia — had crushed their first opponents. Now, players and coaches from those teams were in the first few rows of the stands, watching us file out onto the floor. Cameras were trained on us. Fans shouted out to us in six different languages. "Teen Dream Team! USA!"

As the announcer called my name and I walked out onto the hardwood, I felt goose bumps all down my neck, back, and arms. For the first time since coaches Griffin and McNeil had picked me, I understood what it meant to be one of only ten players representing the United States of America. It was a tremendous ego trip and a very humbling honor, rolled into one exciting package.

We took positions in the middle of the floor for the opening tap. Ten players in shorts and T-shirts. The ref blew the whistle. We froze around the circle. There was a magic moment. And then the ref threw the basketball high into the air and our tournament was underway.

Shawn knocked the opening tap to me, and I took it upcourt and threw an alley-oop pass to Jorge Gonzalez, who swooped through the air to jam it home. Fifteen thousand people roared and hundreds of American flags were waved. I felt good — loose and ready.

It soon became apparent that the guys from Sweden were too slow. I don't mean slow in the usual sense. They were good athletes and in a straight sprint they probably could have kept up with us just fine. But they lacked quickness. Their guards couldn't penetrate and their forwards and center seemed to have ponderously slow first steps. We were up ten points at the end of the first quarter. Twenty-five at the half. Every single one of our starters could beat every single one of their starters off the dribble.

Shawn dunked and dunked again. The fans roared. The basket shook and the backboard quivered.

Jorge blocked half a dozen shots. I could almost hear him say, "Take that stuff out of here!" as he reached up to swat away attempted shots.

Stinger showed off some terrific inside moves. He could score with either hand, going to the basket, moving sideways, or fading away.

I popped from the outside.

And Augustus brought the crowd to its feet time and time again with no-look passes and dazzling slices to the hoop. When Coach Griffin began taking out the starters, toward the end of the first half, we had built a twenty-five point lead and were all playing like a Dream Team.

At the press conference after the game, they asked us about Spain, Germany, Italy, and Croatia. Our coaches had taught us well — there wasn't a single boast or prediction of victory or even moderately cocky remark. Instead, the reporters heard every cliché in the book: "We'll do our best." "We're just honored to be here." "We've seen some of those teams play and we know how good they are." Ray Thompson seemed to be soaking up Italian like a sponge, and I heard him say, "All we can do is give *cento dieci percento!*" One hundred and ten percent!

There was a mood of celebration when we got back to our hotel. Thirty-two teams were now cut to sixteen, and we were on our way. One game down, four more to go. Ernesto, our hotel owner, had sat right behind the

136

team bench, loudly cheering and applauding our efforts. When we got back to his hotel, he threw a little impromptu party for us up on his rooftop terrace. There was a salad and pasta, wine and bread, and vases full of freshly cut flowers from the market in the square below. Other hotel guests joined the festivities, till there were three or four dozen people partying away on the terrace.

A friendly argument broke out between Coach Griffin and Ernesto over whether team members could have glasses of wine. "They're underage," Coach Griffin told him. "Seventeen. Too young to drink alcohol."

"But this is good Italian wine, from Toscana," Ernesto told him.

"I don't doubt the quality. They're just too young."

"Seventeen is already a man," Ernesto said.

"Some of them are sixteen. I'm sorry, but if we break that rule a little bit, we open ourselves up for trouble."

I spotted Ray Thompson off in a corner of the rooftop terrace with his arm around one of the pretty hotel maids. Shawn spotted him, too, and we snuck over to eavesdrop. Ray was describing the victory over Sweden to her in an animated mixture of English and Italian. "So then I flew through the air like an *aeroplano* and dunked the ball with both hands! *Tutt'e due le mani!*" To hear him tell it, he had scored most of our hundred points himself.

"Was that the game I just played in, or did I miss something?" Shawn asked, emerging from the shadows.

"Maybe I looked away, but I don't remember you dunking the ball even with one hand," I chimed in.

Ray scowled. "Anna and I are having a nice, private conversation so why don't you two take your lip action someplace else?"

"Isn't it easier to demonstrate a dunk when you don't have your arm around a girl's back?" I asked.

Ray gave me a look that said, "You wanna mess with me, you're asking for trouble." "You're one to talk," he told me. "I might have to change your nickname from 'Snowman' to 'Snow Romeo.'"

"What are you talking about?"

He smiled at Anna. "Jimmy here is famous for being *innamorato*," and he demonstrated with a couple of kissing sounds, "with Italian women."

Anna laughed, reached out, and ran her fingers through my hair. *"Bello,"* she said.

"Will you please tell me what you're talking about?" I asked Ray again.

"Okay, Snow Romeo. There's a newsstand down beneath this hotel."

"Yeah, I've seen it. It sells Italian papers and magazines."

"They also have *USA Today*," Ray told me. "Actually, yesterday's *USA Today*."

"So what?"

He grinned. "Better hope your girl back home in Granham doesn't have a subscription."

Suddenly it wasn't funny anymore. I backed away, and then began to walk very quickly. It was five flights down to the square, and fifty feet to the green news-stand. I fished out a few thousand lira as I ran, and by the time I reached the stand I held the crumpled bills ready in my hand.

The old woman took my money and handed me a paper, and I rifled through it. Nothing on the front page. Nothing in the middle. I relaxed a little bit. Ray must have been pulling my leg.

Then I reached the back page. There was a big headline. *TEEN DREAM TEAM TAKES ITALY BY STORM!* An article told about the mob scene at our arrival, and about the high expectations for our play. I barely glanced at the words. Instead, my eyes were drawn to three pictures. The first was of Shawn dunking in a practice game. The second showed Augustus shaking hands with the mayor of Rome. And the third showed me at the airport, with my arm around the pretty *signorina* who had asked for my autograph. She had kissed me, but the photographer had taken the shot in such a way that it looked as if I was the aggressor, planting a big smooch right on her lips.

I stood there, in the middle of the bustling flower market, holding the paper with both hands. It was a very big color picture. At least two inches high by one inch wide. The caption beneath it read: *Teen Dream Team member Jimmy Doyle says a big hello to Italy!*

I tried to tell myself that there was nothing to worry about. It had just been in the paper for one day, and Janey never read *USA Today*. Even though she was looking for stories about our team, she would probably never even see it. And even if she did, it was just a harmless accident. The whole thing was kind of comical, really.

I tossed the paper in a trash can and went back up to the party. Everyone was having a great time. Ernesto had put a big wooden barrel on a table and produced a beach ball. A pickup game resembling basketball but with no rules at all had started between my teammates and some of the hotel staff. The rest of the people on the terrace laughed and clapped.

I tried to join the rowdy fun, but my heart wasn't in it. I kept remembering the picture. Tiny print at the top of the article had said it was from a news wire service. Did that mean that other papers might pick up the same story and print the same photograph?

"Hey, what's with the long face?" Coach McNeil asked me. "We won today, remember?"

"Yeah," I said. "I'm just feeling a little . . . tired. Gonna go down to my room and rest."

"Are you sick?"

"I'll probably be back up in a minute. Don't worry."

"I'm not worried," he said. "If I were the coach of our next opponent, I'd be worried."

I went down to my hotel room and made a mental calculation. It would be eleven o'clock in the morning in Minnesota. Janey might be at home. I paced around my room, telling myself how stupid it was to get so worked up about such a ridiculous thing. There was no need to worry. There was certainly no need to make a transatlantic call. Janey knew how I felt about her. Even if somebody showed her the photograph, she would probably just laugh and dismiss it. There was absolutely and positively no need to panic. . . .

I stood still in the middle of the room. Relax. No need to panic. Just a stupid piece of bad luck. Relax . . .

Then I sat down on the bed and grabbed the receiver. The hotel operator put me in touch with an international operator who made the connection. I heard the phone ringing in the Sutherland residence. Even six thousand miles away I could recognize the ring, and I pictured the red phone in their kitchen, hanging just beneath the spice shelf.

A familiar male voice answered. "Hello?"

"Dr. Sutherland? This is Jimmy."

"Calling all the way from Italy?"

"Yes, sir."

"How are you?"

"Very well."

"I'm afraid Janey's not at home."

I hesitated. "Dr. Sutherland, I need to ask you something. A picture of me appeared in a newspaper . . . that looked like something it wasn't. The whole thing was just a stupid mistake and if Janey hasn't seen it there's no reason to even mention it to her, but . . ."

"I'm afraid she's seen it," Dr. Sutherland said.

"But she doesn't read *USA Today* . . ."

"It was a wire-service photo. A number of local papers picked it up. It made the front page of the sports section in the *Minneapolis Star Tribune*."

It felt as if I had been kicked in the stomach. "You're kidding?"

"I told her that kissing is the style of greeting in Europe and you were just being friendly to your hosts," he said. "But most of Janey's friends from school saw the photograph, too, and I guess she was a little hurt."

I stood there, gripping the receiver tightly and shaking my head. "I can't believe this. Just after we stepped off the plane some girl came running up and asked for my autograph. And then she kissed me. I never saw her before. I never saw her again."

"This call is going to cost you a fortune," Dr. Sutherland said. "I'll tell Janey everything you said. You just concentrate on enjoying your vacation in Italy and winning basketball games. Okay?"

I gave him the name and phone number of my hotel in case Janey wanted to call me here, and then we said good-bye and hung up. I lay down on my bed and closed my eyes.

I could imagine what it felt like for Janey to have her friends from school all look at a picture in the newspaper of her boyfriend kissing a pretty Italian girl. In my mind's eye, I recalled the photograph in perfect detail. My arm was around the girl and from the angle it had been taken it looked as if we were locked chin to chin. There's a saying that photographs don't lie, but this one surely did. In real life I had a very clear memory that she had just given me a friendly peck on the cheek.

It probably wouldn't help that the girl in the picture was very cute and was wearing a miniskirt. I stared up at the tiled ceiling. No wonder movie stars and celebrity athletes have trouble keeping their private lives in order. If people follow you around everywhere with cameras, they can probably make you look as bad as they want.

How strange that one stupid photograph taken in an airport in Rome could cause heartache to a sweet girl in Minnesota. Coach McNeil was right — the press can be very dangerous.

CHAPTER FIFTEEN

The Germans were almost as big tournament favorites as we were, and it was bad luck for both teams that we got matched against each other in the second round. One of us would go home early. As soon as the game began it became clear that the Germans had no intention of taking the night train back to Munich.

From the opening basket, they followed a strategy that could be called either extremely competitive or dirty and intimidating, depending on your point of view. Their starters and second stringers were all big, impressively muscled and intense-looking guys who took foul calls without complaining.

When we brought the ball up they trapped aggressively, doubling on the dribbler in the blink of an eye. When we went into our halfcourt offense, they put bodies on our big men and pushed us out of the paint. And when we got a fast break and they needed to foul to prevent a layup, they didn't just make contact but often hammered us.

We started hammering them in return. Players began talking trash back and forth. Flagrant fouls were called against both teams. Opposing coaches and assistants shouted at each other.

It felt more like football or rugby than basketball. A bench-clearing fistfight broke out. Stringer and his German counterpart were thrown out for exchanging punches.

In addition to their constant pressure, the Germans had three secret weapons. One was the tallest player in the tournament. His name was Klaus and he looked as massive as a cathedral as he stood beneath the basket. They also had a forward named Stiller who was just an inch or two shorter than Klaus and had long, thin arms like pipe cleaners that twisted up toward the basket to haul down rebounds again and again.

Shawn couldn't get any easy shots off against these German twin towers. Every time he got the ball inside they collapsed on him, so that he almost seemed to disappear between them. Jorge tried a few fadeaways, but it's difficult to score when you have to do it moving away from the basket.

The third German secret weapon was a guard we sort of dubbed Mr. Perfect because of his movie-star good looks and world-class physique. He wasn't a shooter — I think he only took two or three shots during the entire game. He also wasn't a particularly good passer or ball handler. But the guy had been born to play defense.

They put him on Augustus, and Mr. Perfect shut down our star. He played him defensively the length of the court, with and without the ball. We tried to set screens to give Augustus a little daylight, but Mr. Perfect had a knack for floating around picks like they weren't even there. When Augustus did get the ball and tried to score, Mr. Perfect kept great body position, denying him a first step and a clean look at the hoop.

Then there were the German fans. They were loud to start with, and as it became clear that this game was going to be close and rough, they got louder and louder. Most of them, I'm sure, were just good and loyal fans who had come a long way to cheer on their team, as they had every right to do. I saw many couples and families smiling and waving German flags. But a dozen or so skinheads were sitting just a few rows behind our bench, and they taunted us unmercifully every time we came off the floor for a time-out.

They were scary-looking guys. Many had shaved heads and prominent tattoos, and some wore military paraphernalia or had their faces pierced by needles or pins. I even spotted two or three Nazi swastikas. I don't think I had ever seen anyone wear one in America. Many of the skinheads seemed to know English, and their pronunciation was remarkably clear, which was unfortunate since they were trying to insult us at the top of their lungs.

They were particularly hard on Augustus. "Hey Superstar, only six points!" They hooted and laughed and shouted much more insulting comments at him in English and German.

At first Augustus ignored them, but he was having just about the worst game I had ever seen him play, and their taunts started to get to him. With thirty seconds to go in the first half, we called a time-out. The score was tied and Coach McNeil wanted to make sure we held the ball and worked for one shot. If we made it we would go into the locker room with a lead.

As he diagrammed the play, I saw Augustus glance up at the stands several times. One particularly loud skinhead was riding him unrelentingly. He was a thick-set guy in boots and a military shirt, who sat there hurling abuse and drinking beer he must have smuggled into the arena.

Our huddle broke up. Augustus stood and gave the skinhead a look that should have silenced him. But the skinhead stood up also and laughed and then shouted at him in German. For a moment he and Augustus traded stares.

Then the skinhead launched his can of beer. I think it was mostly empty, but it flew straight and true, catching Augustus on the side of the shoulder. It was the kind of blow that doesn't really hurt, but no athlete likes to have missiles launched at him from the stands. The only question is what you do about it if it happens.

Augustus didn't even hesitate. His first step took him into the second row. His second step took him up to the fourth, where he grabbed the skinhead by the front of his shirt. It all happened so quickly that the skinhead's friends didn't have time to react.

As Augustus and the big guy struggled for grips on the bleacher, a near riot broke out. The other skinheads came to their fellow's aid. Before I even knew what was happening, Augustus's roommate, Jamal, had jumped off our bench and gone to help his friend, and Ray and Shawn weren't far behind.

Coach Griffin tried to break it up, but it took half a dozen Italian security police to restore order. The skinheads were led out of the arena, still laughing and shouting. We walked back onto the floor to finish the half, and then two policemen led us beneath the bleachers to our locker room.

The locker room was very quiet. The fight in the stands and the battle the German team was giving us on the court had both caught us by surprise. We had known the German team was good, but I don't think any of my teammates expected them to play us this rough or this close.

Our coaches, on the other hand, didn't seem particularly surprised. "Chris and I knew ahead of time that there would be games like this," Coach Griffin told us. "We've played enough B-ball against Europeans to know we would come up against guys who were bigger, stronger, and more physical. So we brought our answer to that." He looked at me, and I felt myself swallow.

Coach McNeil jumped in. "Instead of forcing the shot inside we've got to draw the coverage in and then kick the ball back to the perimeter."

It was Coach Griffin's turn to pick up the analysis. "That means kick it out to Snowman. Their two big guys are tied up on Jorge and Shawn, and their super defender is on Augustus. So we just free up our shooting guard and give him some long-range jumpers. If and when they come out to cover him, we move it back inside. But for the first few minutes of the second half, let's give Snowman some shots and let him do his thing."

Two loud knocks sounded on the door. It was the signal that we were to head back out.

"Come on, guys," Coach McNeil said. "Join hands for a minute. Let's go." We formed a big circle. "We're not going to lose this one. It's all character from here on out."

There was a chorus of "Yeah"s and "That's right"s from around the circle.

"Ignore the fans," Coach Griffin told us. "Forget what just happened at the end of the half. Don't be drawn into any more pushing and shoving matches on the floor or in the stands. Just play within yourselves."

The circle seemed to get tighter. Another knock sounded at the door.

"The Teen Dream Team is not gonna fly home at the end of the second round," Shawn said with grim determination.

"Rather die!" Ray muttered.

"Let's get it to Snowman and crack this game wide open!" Jorge said.

Then the door opened and the Italian cop said, " 'Scusate, andiamo?" and we broke the circle of hands and headed back toward the floor.

As we followed the policeman toward the hardwood, Augustus walked next to me for a split second. We had barely exchanged a single word since our nightmare ride through South Central Los Angeles. I figured that he had shown me what he wanted to show me and I had seen what I could see, and if that was enough for him, I wasn't going to try to push a possible friendship any further. Now he said simply, "You're the man, Snow-man."

There were a lot of boos as the crowd caught a glimpse of us. I guess the Germans and some of the Italians didn't like the fact that Augustus had gone up into the stands after a fan. The Teen Dream Team had sure lost its popularity in a hurry. *"Mascalzoni!"* *"Schweinen!"* "Go back to America!"

Shawn managed to win the opening tap and we took the ball up on offense. It was clear that the Germans were following the same defensive strategy that had worked for them in the first half. Their two big men set up camp under our basket. Mr. Perfect shadowed Augustus, and got help from their two guards.

That left me pretty free. I floated around the perimeter.

We worked the ball in to Jorge. Their whole team collapsed around him, anticipating a move to the hoop. Instead, Jorge kicked it back out to me a foot or two beyond the three-point line. I set my feet and let fly. A long three-pointer is a thing of beauty. It begins with a snap of the wrist. Then a long arc. It ends with a swish.

The Germans took the ball down and tried a jump-shot. As soon as I saw their shot go up, I began sprinting the other way. Shawn rebounded and tossed me a football bomb of a pass. I had to turn on all of the jets to catch it, but once I did it was a pretty easy thing just to lay it up.

The next time we had the ball, we got it to Augustus, who dribbled it into the corner as if setting up for a jumper. Mr. Perfect and another guard doubled on him. Once again he kicked it way back to me. I was feeling the rhythm now. The howls of the crowd were a faraway buzz. The TV cameras were out of it. Worries about Janey being mad at me were momentarily forgotten. I caught the pass and stepped back behind the three-point line. I found the hoop with my eyes. Locked onto the orange circle. Put the ball up. Snap. Arc. Swish. Nothing but net.

After that the Germans started covering me, but in a way it was too late. My eight-point burst got us going, and our other players caught fire. When the Germans spread their defense to cover me, it let Augustus penetrate and freed our big men up for occasional Teen Dream Team Funka-Dunka Slammas!

We won by twelve points. Compared to the first half, the second half was a peace conference. There were no fights, and very little trash talking. After the game, the Germans came over and congratulated us. They were very disappointed, but I was really impressed by their sportsmanship. "You were the difference today," Klaus, the giant, told me, shaking my hand. "Great shooting."

"Thanks. This was a tough game."

"You will win all the rest," he told me. "Except maybe for Spain. They are very strong, too. Good luck."

The postgame press conference was held in a big and windowless room near our locker room. We tried to focus on our own playing and sound humble, as we had been taught, but it had been a rough game with lots of controversial incidents and the questions were difficult and critical.

"Why did you throw the first punch in the fight?" a reporter with a British accent asked Stinger.

"I don't know who punched who first," he replied. "There was a lot of pushing and shoving in that first half. I'm sorry for my part of what happened."

Next, an Italian reporter went after Coach McNeil. "We saw you and the German coach shouting at each other. Two times you crossed the coaches' line. Is this the way to set a model for young players?"

"Everyone who plays basketball or coaches it gets a little hot now and then," he answered. "The German coach did a great job. If we traded a few sharp words during the game, it didn't mean anything."

A young German reporter stepped forward and jabbed out his finger toward Coach McNeil. "But the behavior of the coach affects the players, *ja?* For you, maybe it was just words, but one of your players ran up into the stands."

"That fight in the stands had absolutely nothing to do with Coach McNeil," Augustus told him. "A punk threw something at me and I defended myself."

There were half a dozen German reporters in the room, and they didn't seem to want to let it drop so easily. "You say he threw something at you," a woman reporter said. "But you only had six points in the first half. Maybe your poor playing made you angry?"

"I've had poor shooting nights before," Augustus told her. "They're part of the game. No big deal."

The young German reporter who had spoken first stepped a bit closer to us and raised his voice. He was dressed more casually than the other reporters, and from his tone it was clear that he didn't think too much of Augustus.

I guess this is where my story begins to get just a little bit hard to believe. After all, it was a stupid basketball press conference in a windowless room beneath a concrete arena, and we were just sixteen and seventeen years old and well coached to be on our best behavior. But on one side, this young German reporter seemed to be trying to create controversy. And on the other side, I had gotten to know Augustus a little bit — I had seen where he came from and how that background had given him some pretty strong political views — so I wasn't completely surprised when things started to swing wildly out of control.

"You are from Los Angeles, correct?" the young German reporter asked. Augustus looked back at him and slowly nodded. "Everyone knows you have a problem with violence there. We have seen on TV the riots and gang shootings and white people being pulled from their automobiles and beaten up. So maybe for you, running into the stands to punch someone is no big deal . . . ?"

"I think we've heard enough. . . ." Coach Griffin cut him off, trying to wrap up the press conference before things got out of hand. But Augustus was staring right at the reporter, and when he began to answer, Coach Griffin let him speak.

"Everywhere I go in Rome I see homeless black men on the street, selling clothes and jewelry for whatever they can get," he said in a loud, clear voice. Cameras flashed. There was a buzz from the Italian reporters. Augustus didn't even blink — he just looked out over the throng and continued. "The rest of this country looks rich and very comfortable, but not the African brothers."

Augustus lowered his gaze till he was staring right into the eyes of the reporter. "And you're not the only one who watches world news on TV. I've seen a lot about Germany, too. Punks like the one tonight marching against foreigners, burning down their homes, and even trying to kill them. That guy I went after was wearing a swastika. So if we have problems in L.A., it sounds to me like you Germans have problems, too. Like maybe the old Nazi days are threatening to come back."

The young reporter looked up at him. "You are speaking from ignorance."

A look came into Augustus's eyes that I had seen once before. "Say what? You calling me ignorant?"

"Ignorant of Germany. *Ja.* You should just try to play basketball. . . ."

I don't think Augustus meant to attack the reporter

but he definitely meant to confront him. He stepped forward, and the German reporter stepped forward, and the next thing I knew everybody seemed to be holding and pushing everybody, except for a dozen or so Italian policemen who stood idly by, watching the whole thing as if it were some kind of comic opera.

To this day I'm not sure how our coaches got us out of that room so fast and back on our team bus. Things were kind of quiet as our driver worked his way through the crowded streets of Rome. At one point, as we neared our hotel, Augustus stood up and said he'd like to apologize to all of us and especially to our coaches for losing his cool.

Coach Griffin waved him down. "You don't have to apologize," he said. "You had every reason to go up into the stands. Anybody throws something at me, I might go after him, too. As for the reporter, the guy was a jerk, and you answered him from the heart. I agreed with everything you said in there."

Coach McNeil nodded. "Me, too." He paused. "I just hope this thing dies down so that we can concentrate on basketball."

CHAPTER SIXTEEN

The day after the victory against the German team began normally enough. We woke up at seven, put on our sweats, met for juice, toast, and fruit, and then jogged two miles to the high school gym where we had our workouts. Everyone was sore from the previous day's bruising game, and there were a lot of grunts and groans as we ran through the narrow cobblestone streets. A small crowd was waiting for us in front of the gym. I was afraid we might have alienated some people with all the mayhem in the game against the Germans, but these people were fans who wanted to snap pictures and get autographs.

Practice itself was pretty normal, too. We had to work hard not to let down psychologically. There was a tendency to think that we had conquered one of the giants of the tournament, and that our next game would be easier. "Every game's the same," Coach McNeil told us. "We play them all with everything we've got."

We jogged back to the hotel, showered in our rooms, and had a free hour till lunch. As soon as I got back to the hotel I did what I had done for the past two days — check at the desk for messages from Janey. The clerk knew me by now, and he just shook his head as I got close. "No messages from America."

I was tempted to try to call her, but it was very early in the morning in America and she would be fast asleep. Anyway, what was the point? I had told Dr. Sutherland the whole story, and I was sure he had relayed it to her very persuasively. I kept reminding myself that I hadn't done anything wrong. If one of us was guilty of something, it was Janey for being too jealous. She should have known that the picture in the paper must have been an accident. She should have trusted me.

I paced up and back, in the small hotel room. It was her problem. Not mine. Up and back. Shawn took off his headphones and glared at me. "You're making me dizzy," he said. "What's the problem?"

"Nothing."

"You're acting like a psycho."

"Sorry. Maybe I'll take a walk."

"We're not supposed to leave the square," he reminded me.

"I just need to get out of this room."

"Your problem is that you never learned to appreciate sleep," Shawn said. "Sleep in daylight is even sweeter than sleep in darkness." As I left the room I saw him roll over onto his stomach, close his eyes, and assume that blissful snoozing position that I knew would soon lead him to the land of bulldozer snores.

I headed down into the square. Right outside our hotel was a fish cart. There were squids and octopuses, and sections of giant swordfish, which they call *pesce spada*. The head of the *pesce spada*, with its protruding two-foot sword, had the place of honor at the front of the cart. Tiny flies buzzed around its eyes.

I walked on. The vegetable carts were my favorite. Just by walking by them it was possible to tell how fresh the produce was. The tomatoes didn't look nearly as red as the ones in America, but when you bit into a tomato from one of these stalls, a wonderfully zesty taste exploded in your mouth. There were eggplants and squash flowers, wild greens and fresh figs.

Beyond the vegetables I came to the flowers. The old women who sold flowers from these carts smiled at me. *"Fiori per la tua ragazza,"* they called out with toothy grins. I knew that they were suggesting that I buy flowers for a girlfriend, and if Janey had been in Italy a few of their roses might have disappeared from the stalls pretty quickly. But Janey was in Minnesota and I was in Rome.

We weren't supposed to leave the square without getting permission, but we had been staying at Campo dei Fiori long enough to know our way around the narrow streets that snaked away from the market. Our coaches had relaxed a little bit on this particular rule. I followed one of the cobblestone streets at random, stopping now and then to admire little courtyard gardens and terraces.

The thing I liked most about Rome is the way each and every street has its own secret art masterpieces. Tiny statues at the entrances to buildings, stonework above doorways, hundreds-of-years-old fountains half hidden in shadowy corners — beautiful surprises lay in wait for me every thirty or forty feet.

I had just about decided to turn back when I saw a florist. This wasn't a little stall like the ones out in the market, but rather a big and modern shop. Stickers in the window showed that they took credit cards and travelers checks, and a small sign proclaimed, ENGLISH, JAPANESE, OK.

A thought came to me. At first I tried to dismiss it because of the expense, but it wasn't the kind of thought you can get rid of easily. I peered in the window. Two young women and an older man were at work pruning flowers and making up bouquets. The shop had a nice feel to it. The older man felt my glance through the window. He looked up, smiled, and waved for me to enter.

The inside of the shop smelled sweet with natural perfume from the thousands of blossoms. *"Si?"* the man said.

"Do you speak English?"

"Maria, *aiuto.*"

One of the young women came over, wiping her wet hands on a towel. "Yes?"

"I'd like to know how much it costs to send a dozen red roses to someone in America."

The young woman smiled. Her English was quite good. "We don't send them from Italy," she said. "We wire to a store in the city in America where you're sending them. So they arrive fresh and beautiful. Where are

159

you sending them?" I told her and she flipped through a couple of thick books. "Yes, we can arrange it for you." She named an amount a little less than a hundred dollars.

"That's more than I can afford," I told her. "But thanks anyway."

I started walking out of the shop. *"Aspetti,"* the man said. "Wait." He began conversing with the young woman in fast Italian. I kind of guessed that he was asking her what I had wanted, and what the problem was. When he understood, he turned back to me and smiled. "Teen Dream Team?"

I nodded, surprised.

He picked up an Italian newspaper, opened to the sports section, and showed me a picture of myself launching a jumpshot. "Doyle," he read. "Jimmy Doyle." He looked at me. *"Fiori per la tua ragazza?"* He thumped his heart to show that he was asking if the flowers were for my true love.

I kind of blushed and nodded. The two young women giggled.

"Special price," he said, and named a lower amount.

It was still more than seventy dollars. I had brought a grand total of two hundred dollars spending money with me from my small savings account back in Granham. It seemed crazy to spend more than a third of it for a dozen roses.

The old man was smiling at me, waiting for me to agree. I was a little embarrassed. "I really can't. Thank you," I said, and hurried out of his store. I walked back to our hotel, reassuring myself that I had done the right thing. My two hundred dollars had already dwindled to about a hundred and sixty. And I needed to buy presents for Mom and my sisters and Janey. There was no way I could spend seventy on one silly bouquet of roses.

Janey might not even like them. I kept reminding myself that I hadn't done anything wrong and so I didn't owe her anything.

As I walked up the stairs to my hotel floor, I could hear Shawn snoring away in our room. I let myself in quietly. He was flat on his back, eyes closed and mouth wide open, making sounds like the world's biggest wind tunnel.

Thirty minutes till lunch. I lay down on my bed and shut my eyes. There was no use worrying about it — wiring flowers across the Atlantic was out of my spending range. Anyway, it might be dangerous to appear to be apologizing when I hadn't done anything wrong. If anything, Janey should send me roses for putting me through this. The wind tunnel a few feet away increased in volume. I opened my eyes and stared up at the ceiling, in case Shawn's snoring shook loose a few tiles.

Seventy dollars. There were a lot of better things to spend the money on. I tried to think of a few, without much success. After a minute or two I got out of bed.

My money was with my passport in a small belt pack that I kept at the bottom of my suitcase. I fished out seventy dollars, three twenties and a ten. The remaining bills formed a very small pile indeed. My mother and sisters would have to be satisfied with inexpensive presents. Maybe I could get them snazzy T-shirts.

I hurried downstairs and back to the flower shop. The old man greeted me with a handshake and a big smile. I gave him my American money and he looked up the current exchange rate and nodded that it would be just enough. "Roses?" he asked.

"Red roses," I told him, and pointed to some to make sure we were connecting.

He gave me a card to fill out, and I wrote down Janey's address and phone number. There was a space on the card marked *messaggi*. "Please write the words that you would like to send with the flowers," the young woman told me.

I thought of about ten messages, and rejected them. Some were stupid. Others sounded funny to me, but they might not sound funny to her. A few were too apologetic — I reminded myself that I really hadn't done anything wrong.

The young woman was sitting ten feet away, trimming a tiny orange tree and watching me. When I glanced at her, she smiled. "It's difficult, yes?"

"Very," I agreed. And then I brought the card over to her and asked in a whisper, "How do you say, 'I love you,' in Italian?"

She smiled and took the pen from me. I guess she could tell that I didn't want everyone in the store to know I was sending such a soppy message. She tore off a piece of gray paper that they wrap bouquets in, and wrote *Ti amo*. I copied the two words onto the card in

162

my own hand. The young woman nodded. "Nice flowers," she said. "Nice message. *Belissimo.*"

The old man assured me that Janey would get the flowers within forty-eight hours, and wished me good luck in the tournament. We shook hands and then I was out of the store and back on the cobblestone street, poorer but with peace of mind.

I guess maybe when you love someone and there's a misunderstanding, it doesn't matter who's at fault. What matters is to reach out and try to set things right as soon as possible. I got a lot of pleasure imagining Janey's face when the roses arrived, and when she guessed the meaning of the Italian words. All in all, it seemed like seventy dollars well spent.

I was so wrapped up with these happy thoughts that I didn't see Coach McNeil until he was about thirty feet away from me. He waved and headed right for me, and I surprised to see that he was with two Italian policemen. "Finally, Snowman," he said. "I've been looking all over for you. I don't mind that you left the square, but you should have told your roommate where you were going."

"Sorry," I replied. "He was asleep and I wasn't going very far." I glanced at the policemen. They weren't normal cops. Both of them carried what looked like submachine guns. "Is something wrong?"

"Very."

Something about the way he said that one word made me kind of snap to attention. "What? Anything I did?"

He shook his head. "Nothing anybody did. Come on.

We'll talk about it back in the hotel. Everyone else is waiting there." And we headed back to Campo dei Fiori at high speed, with the two gun-toting policemen trailing us on either side.

CHAPTER SEVENTEEN

Coach McNeil introduced him as Mr. Sullivan from the American diplomatic corps, but the man looked as if he belonged in a James Bond film. He was tall, handsome, dressed in a dark suit, and he gave off a kind of quiet confidence. When he moved, I could see that he was a natural athlete. He was a little bit too muscular and heavy-footed for a basketball player. If I had to guess, I would have said his thing was hand-to-hand combat.

We met in Ernesto's office, on the first floor of the hotel. It was an elegant room with leather-bound account books on shelves on one wall and a handsome antique wood desk near the windows. I think the room faced out onto the square, but the drapes were all drawn so it was impossible to tell. A policeman with a submachine gun stood at the door.

Mr. Sullivan walked to the front of the office and began to speak in prairie-flat tones that reminded me of the people back home. "Your game against Germany last night was seen all over Europe," he began. "The TV ratings were much higher than anyone expected. The fistfight in the game, the fight in the bleachers, and the press conference after the game were carried live and played again and again on late night and early morning German news shows. The whole thing led to stories in several of the major German newspapers."

He lifted a few newspapers off a table to show us. There were indeed large headlines in German and pictures of Augustus grappling with the skinhead in the stands and walking toward the reporter in the briefing room.

"It's not so much what you said or did that got so much attention," he told Augustus. "That reporter who provoked you isn't taken very seriously by his colleagues — he works for a right-wing paper and it's surprising this tournament even gave him press credentials. No, it's the timing that's caused so much trouble. The political situation in Germany vis-a-vis foreigners and refugees is a powder keg right now. With your comments getting such attention, someone saw a golden opportunity to grab publicity and maybe push America around a little."

Mr. Sullivan put the newspapers back on the table and took a breath. "This morning a death threat was called in to *La Repubblica*, a major Roman newspaper, against you," he told Augustus. "Actually, it was against the whole team." A long second ticked off as we looked at each other. It didn't seem real, but it only took one look at Mr. Sullivan's face to know that something very serious had indeed happened. "The caller claimed to be from a radical neo-Nazi group we're familiar with. I don't think it would be stretching it to call them terrorists. Like all terrorists they crave publicity, and a stunt like this, where they can take a shot at intimidating the United States of America, is perfect for them."

"So you think they're just doing it to get attention?" Augustus asked.

"It's probably just a scare tactic, to try to get your team to withdraw from the tournament. If they really wanted to hurt you, they wouldn't have called the newspaper first. They would have just come after you." Mr. Sullivan hesitated. "But at the same time, we can't entirely dismiss it."

It's not a very good feeling when the guy who is telling you that a death threat may be for real is a cool and knowledgeable professional. "The group that called in the threat is certainly capable of committing a violent act," Mr. Sullivan said. "And we have some intelligence information that I can't go into in any depth, except to say that it's a little worrying. It sort of forces our hand, in the sense that we have to assume the worst. Which brings us to the question of what to do. You need to meet as a team, but first I'd better give you the government's position."

Mr. Sullivan squared his shoulders — he seemed somehow a bit more stiff and official-looking when he began to speak for the U.S. government. "The ambassador asked me to tell you that if you want to stay and finish the tournament, he will personally see to your safety. We don't like the idea of a team of young people representing the United States of America being threatened on foreign soil, and we have the capability here in Rome to protect you.

"This hotel is wide open to the square and we can't control the traffic of guests, so we'll have to move all of you into fully secure housing. The Italian government has already offered to help us guard you. Such precautions are probably unnecessary, but if you decide to stay and play we intend to take very good care of you. On the other hand, if you guys want to go home, no one will hold it against you. It's no fun to live and practice and play under a death threat. So I guess it's your decision. Now I better turn things over to your coaches."

Coaches Griffin and McNeil walked to the front of the room. Neither of them seemed to know quite what to say. "Well, this just beats all," Coach McNeil finally muttered. "Twenty-six years I've been around basketball and I thought I'd seen everything, but this is a new one." He looked out at us, his gaze moving from face to face. "There are two ways of thinking about it. One way is that we have a job to do here: We're representing the United States of America. I'm as patriotic as the next guy, and I've never been one to let a bully push me off a playground.

"The other way is that you guys are all minors. Our government and the Italian government can make all the noises they want about protecting you, but if you want to go home, or your parents want you home, you should go. Right away. Without a second thought. You don't owe anything to anyone. We can probably get you flights tonight or tomorrow morning."

Coach Griffin nodded. "I guess the thing to do now is to send you back to your rooms. Take an hour to think, while you pack your bags. Call home and talk to your parents. The team will pick up the charge of the calls, so don't worry about that. After an hour Coach McNeil and I will come around and talk to you, room by room. And listen — nobody tries to influence anyone else to stay. It's a personal and a family decision. Okay?"

We nodded, and headed up to our rooms. The hotel seemed to be crawling with Italian police. Soon Shawn and I were alone in our room, with our suitcases on our beds. "What do you think, Snowman?" he asked.

"I don't know," I said. "I'm kind of numb."

"Want to call home first?"

"No, you go. Should I give you privacy?"

He shrugged. "Don't bother. I'm just calling to tell them what's going down. I make my own decisions, and I already made up my mind down in that office. I'm gonna hang with my homey."

He called home and described the whole situation to his parents in terms that made it sound a lot less dangerous than it really was. "They think it's just a bunch of kooks, Ma. Some kind of publicity stunt. They're going to be guarding us 'round the clock, so there's nothing to worry about."

When he was done, I called my mom. It was seventhirty in the morning in Granham and I got her at home, just before she left for the store. "Something weird's happening here," I told her.

"I know," she said. "I just saw it on CNN."

"You're kidding!"

"Jimmy, I'm scared. Are you going to come home?"

I hadn't made up my mind till she asked the question, but suddenly I heard myself repeating almost word for word what Shawn had said. "The police think it's just kooks. They're going to protect us. I came here to represent the United States of America and I want to stay and do that."

"Will you be very careful?"

"Extremely," I promised her. "Can I stay?"

There were a few seconds of silence. "You're old enough to make your own decision. Just take care, my baby."

"Don't worry, Mom. I'll be back home in Granham before you know it. 'Bye. I love you." It wasn't until after I hung up that I realized I hadn't asked about Janey. Well, I had sent the roses and done what I could, and now I had to worry about myself. I began packing at high speed.

Ten minutes later a loud knock exploded against our door. Shawn and I both jerked around, and then caught ourselves and smiled, a little embarrassed at being so much on edge. "Friend or foe?" I called out.

"Coaches," a familiar voice said, and then Griffin and McNeil entered the room. "How's the packing going, guys?"

"Almost done," Shawn told them.

"You have a chance to call home?"

We both nodded.

"To take the pressure off, let me tell you now that at least three of your teammates have decided to go home.

170

Actually, I think it was their parents who made the decision. But they're going."

"Who?" Shawn asked.

"Patterson, Hayes, and Raymond."

"Ray?" Shawn asked, surprise ringing clearly in his voice.

"He's an only child, and his mother is not well. His parents can't stand the idea of his being in any danger. I don't blame them one bit for wanting him home. Ray doesn't want to go, but we're sending him stateside tonight."

"So there's no shame in going home," Coach McNeil added. "None at all. What are you guys gonna do?"

"I'm hanging," Shawn said.

"You're sure?" Coach McNeil asked him. "You talked to your parents and they agree?"

"One hundred percent."

There was a momentary silence in the high-ceilinged hotel room as the two coaches and Shawn looked at me.

"Me, too," I heard myself whisper. "I wanna win this tournament."

"Your mom knows what's happening?" Coach Griffin asked me. "I was the one who called her and talked to her about this tournament, so I feel sort of responsible for your coming here."

"She knows. She said the decision about staying is up to me."

"Even if she said that, think about it again, Jimmy. I know that it's just your mom and your two sisters at home. Your mother sounded like a sweet and gentle lady. If you stay, with the threat and all, it could be hard on her."

I looked back at him and felt myself smile. "You may have talked to my mom but you don't know her. If she said it was up to me, then it's up to me. She sounds sweet and timid on the phone, but she's the strongest woman in Minnesota."

CHAPTER EIGHTEEN

Patterson, Hayes, and Ray said good-bye to us in the hotel lobby.

The American Embassy had helped get them flights back to America almost immediately. They seemed to have very different reactions to going back. Patterson hadn't played more than three minutes in our first two games, and I think he was pretty relieved to be getting out of this mess. He shook hands with all of us and then picked up his suitcase and headed out to a police car that was all set to whisk them to the airport. Hayes seemed a bit more reluctant to leave, but he said his good-byes and followed Patterson out.

Ray clearly didn't want to go. In fact, he was almost in tears. "I wanna hang," he kept saying. "I *am* the Teen Dream Team. There are *signorinas* ready to climb in my window and in two more weeks I could learn this language." Bitterness rang in his voice. "My folks just don't understand. They're doing this for themselves, not for me."

We all told him that we didn't blame him, and that there was nothing he could do. "I started all this trouble, but if my aunt told me to come home, I'd be on that plane with you," Augustus told him.

"That's right," Shawn said, putting a hand on Ray's shoulder. "We know you're hanging with us in spirit."

"Damn," Ray repeated several times. He wiped a few tears away with the back of his wrist. "Damn it!"

An Italian policeman spoke to Coach Griffin, who nodded and approached us. "Ray, you gotta go," he said. "With the afternoon traffic and all, they gotta leave right now for you to make the flight."

"So if I hang here a few more minutes, they might miss it and I'd have to stay?" he asked. It wasn't much of a joke, but it was the last one our team comedian made in Italy. He took a deep breath, and then said good-bye to us one after the other. "Shine on, star," he told Augustus. "Be tough, big man," he told Shawn. He came to me, and managed a smile. "Snowman, turns out you shoot the ball pretty good for a short white guy. Ice them, baby."

"I will," I promised him. "Listen, don't be too angry with your parents. It sounds like, for some reason I don't understand, they actually like you a little bit."

He nodded and went on down the row, giving hugs and slapping hands. When he was done, he wiped his eyes a final time, picked up his bag, and headed for the police car. He got in and almost immediately the car pulled away from the curb. Its siren began to shriek and its light flashed as it headed out of the square.

A pall of glumness settled over us with Ray's departure. He may not have been a starter, but he had been the heart and soul of our team. His jokes and pranks kept us loose. Now he, Hayes, and Patterson were on their way back to America, and there were just seven of us left.

A long black limousine pulled up outside the hotel, flanked by Italian police cars and several cops on motorcycles. "This is a scene right out of *The Godfather*," Shawn muttered.

"Just precautions to get you out of this hotel safely," Mr. Sullivan said. "As I mentioned, there's some intelligence information that concerns us just a little." He looked out the door, waiting for some kind of signal. "When I say go, we head straight for the limo," he told us. "Leave your bags by the back trunk and we'll load them in for you."

Ernesto walked out from his office to wave good-bye to us. "I will be watching you in the tournament," he said. "Come back and stay here again, when things are less crazy."

Outside the hotel, Italian policemen pushed a crowd of onlookers back about thirty yards from the doors. Two men who I took to be security agents got out of the limo. Both were tall, broad shouldered, and dressed like Mr. Sullivan in dark suits. Sunglasses hid their eyes. One wore some kind of headset with a microphone. He spoke into the microphone, nodded, and then waved for us to come. "Okay, guys," Mr. Sullivan said. "Let's go!"

Stinger was the first out. I was third. It was a very strange thing to step out into daylight and feel that someone might be aiming a gun at me or getting ready to heave a bomb in my direction. I walked very quickly. Behind me, Mr. Sullivan himself escorted Augustus toward the limo.

Following directions, I dropped my suitcase near the back trunk and got in the door. It felt surprisingly good to get out of the public view — out of the sunlight. I realized that I had been holding my breath, and let it out. Stinger shot me a sympathetic grin. "This is weird," I whispered.

"Don't like it much myself," he agreed.

As soon as the last player was in and the last bag stowed, our big limo set off through the narrow streets of Rome with a police escort clearing the way as best they could. People didn't seem to get out of the way for police sirens in Italy the way they do in America. A few motorists went right on driving in the center of the road, refusing to budge until the police practically bumped them from behind.

The trip took nearly an hour. We left the flower markets, food stalls, and picturesque streets of Campo dei Fiori far behind, and entered a drab neighborhood of endless suburbs. Our limo finally stopped at the gate of what looked like a cross between a small hotel and a military compound. The four-story building was set far back from the street and surrounded by barbed wire. Most of its windows were completely obscured by a dense green wall of trees and tall hedges.

We each got our own room. It was a comfortable enough place — kind of like a Holiday Inn — except that it had a distinctly military feel. No one ever told us exactly what the building was, or who owned and operated it. As I unpacked my stuff in my little third-floor room, I thought that they weren't telling us very much. For example, who exactly had made the death threat? And what was this inside intelligence information that had prompted them to move us out of our hotel?

That evening after dinner, we got a surprise visit from three dignitaries: the American ambassador, a United States senator who happened to be visiting Italy, and the mayor of Rome. They all came together, just in time to drink coffee and eat dessert with us. A camera crew and several photographers arrived with them. Apparently we had become big enough media figures for such a powerful threesome to seek us out.

We had met the mayor of Rome once before, when we first arrived and visited his office. He was a friendly man who spoke English with a thick accent. "So what was for dinner?" he asked, looking around as our mostly empty plates were cleared away. "Ah, I see — Lasagna. *Buone?*"

"*Molto buone,*" we all said back to him.

He smiled, very pleased. "I don't know much about basketball, but your Italian is getting better."

The American ambassador was a short, dapper-looking man in his middle fifties with a knack for remembering people's names. Coach McNeil went down the table introducing us one by one, and for the rest of the meeting the ambassador called us by our names without further prompting. He appeared to defer to the senator whenever one of them had to make a decision or answer a question.

I had never met anyone as important as a United States senator before, and I watched him closely as he settled his bulk in a chair. He was a big, round-shouldered man with a bald head and bushy eyebrows. I don't know much about expensive clothes, but he must have been wearing several thousand dollars' worth of wool suit and cotton shirt and silk tie.

"I'm very glad you fellows decided to stay," the senator began. He poked a piece of cake suspiciously with a fork and apparently decided not to eat it. "Of course this whole thing's very unfortunate, but the thing to do is to hang tough. Lots of people are watching you."

"While you're hanging tough, we're going to try to make sure you have as good a time as possible under the circumstances," the ambassador added.

"Will we get to see the Colosseum?" Stinger asked him. "I've been waiting on that."

"Sightseeing will have to be curtailed, at least around Rome," the ambassador said. "But we'll try to arrange some activities for you here. I'm sure a few videos can be brought in. And I understand there's a lounge with a Ping-Pong table and pinball machines."

"If they came all the way to Rome to see our Colosseum, they must see it!" the mayor of Rome jumped in enthusiastically. Of the three men, he seemed to me by far the most genuine. "Maybe a private visit can be arranged, after tourist hours. You all want to go, yes?"

We all nodded.

"I will see what I can do," he promised.

"What about our practices?" Augie asked. "We need to stay sharp."

"We'll provide safe transportation to practices and games, Augustus," the ambassador assured him. "I understand that there's a gym not too far from here which will be perfect for your needs." He took a sip of coffee. Next to him the senator glanced at his watch. "Anything else?"

I took a deep breath. "Mr. Sullivan, the security agent who talked to us at the hotel, told us that there was some reason for thinking the death threat against us might be for real. And since you've obviously gone to a lot of trouble and expense to move us all here and guard us so carefully, I was kind of wondering what that reason was?"

The ambassador glanced at the senator. They both looked a little uncomfortable. "Jim, that's classified intelligence information," the ambassador said.

"I don't mean to make trouble, sir," I went on, "but since we're the ones at risk, don't you think we have a right to know?"

The two of them thought about it for a second and then the senator smiled and took control. "We both completely agree with you, but that doesn't mean we can tell you." He leaned forward, as if confiding a great secret. "See, boys, one of the problems with a job like ours, where you have access to classified information, is that you must follow certain rules. Now I could tell you a little about this threat business, but it's better for all of you if I don't say anything. You know the old saying, 'A little knowledge is a dangerous thing.' I don't want to spook you."

"Speaking for myself," I told him, "I think I'd rather know. Even a little bit."

"Yeah," Jorge agreed. "We're the ones in danger."

"If we all knew a little more, maybe we could be careful to avoid certain things," Coach McNeil suggested.

Once again, the senator and the ambassador exchanged glances. The senator sat back, and the ambassador seemed to take this as a signal for him to handle things. "I can't get too specific," he told us. "But you'll notice that at all your tournament games from now on, there'll be metal detectors at the doors. Police will be checking out the crowd. They'll be looking for one man whose face we know. We have reason to think he's in Italy. Perhaps even in Rome. And that's really all either of us can tell you."

"You mustn't worry — we will keep you safe," the mayor promised us. "These things happen from time to time. We know how to deal with them."

The senator glanced at his watch again, and pushed the plate of cake away. "I'm afraid we need to be heading off in a few seconds."

He stood up, dabbed his lips with a napkin, fixed his silk tie, and cleared his throat. The cameramen, who up till now had merely wolfed down cake and coffee, seemed to take these actions as cues to get ready. "Boys," the senator said, spreading out his arms to include all of us, "this despicable terrorist threat is getting a lot of press all over the world."

Cameras began to whir and flash, recording his little speech from different angles. "Your friends and families back home are worried about you, but let me tell you something — they're also damn proud! You came here with a job to do." He paused for dramatic effect. "Threats made by cowards don't frighten us. We're not going anywhere, are we?" When it became clear that he wasn't going to get a response from any of us, he supplied his own bombastic answer. "Hell no! We're gonna win this tournament for the good old U. S. of A!"

He walked down the table, putting his hand on each one of our shoulders. "The Italians are our trusted allies. The mayor, here, is a good friend. We feel safe and comfortable in Rome. No matter what the threat, our red, white, and blue colors don't run!" I saw one of the cameramen give him a little hand signal, and he began speaking a tiny bit faster. "So remember, boys, from Los Angeles to Manhattan, from Fairbanks to Honolulu, everyone's behind you. The president himself is following this story and wishes you well. I want to assure your families that we'll do what it takes to protect you. Good luck, play hard, and God bless the United States of America!"

He ended up right behind Augustus, with his hands on Augustus's shoulders, and a smile frozen on his face for about ten seconds. I could tell that the whole act really pissed Augustus off. Finally the senator stepped away. "Get it?" he asked, wiping his bald head with a white handkerchief.

"Bingo," the head cameraman replied.

"Okay," he said, "then we're out of here. 'Bye, boys. Come on Arthur, Marco. We can just make that hospital ribbon cutting." He headed for the door at high speed.

The ambassador's voice floated back to us from just outside the door. "It's not a hospital ribbon cutting — it's the awards ceremony for the American Club's dog show."

"Whatever. Where the hell's my limo?"

Then they were gone. We all looked at each other. There was a very long and angry silence. Jamal spoke first. "If they show that senator's speech on TV, who-ever's out there'll shoot us for sure."

Heads nodded around the table. "We were used," Shawn rumbled.

There came a loud chorus of agreement.

"Used and abused."

"What a phony."

"Our necks are on the line, and he's fishing for votes."

Coach Griffin raised his arm to quiet everyone. "You're right," he said. "We were used and abused." He frowned. "But to tell you the truth, I don't know how to avoid it. We're kind of at the mercy of the powers that are now protecting us. I guess we have been ever since our sports trip to Italy became politicized."

"Maybe the moral is that people as young as you guys are shouldn't play international sports," Coach

McNeil said. "Maybe in this day and age it doesn't work. Too intense pressure. Too much politics. So many things can go wrong."

Anthony Bell, the reserve from Philadelphia, surprised all of us by suddenly calling out, "Just basketball."

Our two coaches looked at him. We all did. He had never spoken out at a team meeting before.

He said it again. "From now on, just basketball."

"That's right, Bell," Jamal Stokes agreed. "You got it. Just hoop."

"Yeah, that's why we came here. To play," Shawn shouted out. "Hoop."

"To play ball."

"To win."

"No more politics."

"Bell's right. From now on no more talking — just hoop!"

Augustus sat quietly, listening to this clamor for pure sports — separate from politics — without joining in. I wondered whether he took his teammates' comments as a rebuke to him for getting this whole mess started in the first place. Or did he remain quiet because he thought we were foolish? I knew how strong his opinions were, and that he thought just about everything had a political and a racial side to it.

Our impromptu team meeting broke up an hour or so before bedtime. We played a few games of Ping-Pong in the lounge, and soon guys started heading back to their rooms. It had been a stressful day, and I guess everyone was a little tired.

My room seemed even smaller than I remembered it. The bathroom was tiny. I washed and brushed and got into bed. I always sleep with the window open, but as I lay there with the moon shining in through the open curtain, I got the creeps. What if someone was out there? The man the ambassador had mentioned . . . the one with the gun. What if he was climbing one of the trees outside this building?

I knew my fears were stupid, and that my imagination was running wild, but I couldn't help myself. There had never been anyone who had wanted to kill me before. I got up, closed and latched the window, and drew the curtains. The room felt stuffy, but a little safer. I lay down again and closed my eyes. Soon, I found myself wondering about the door. I was pretty sure I had locked it. I opened my eyes and glanced at it. Whether I had locked it or not, I certainly hadn't drawn the chain.

A minute passed. Maybe two. I reminded myself that there was a guard post just outside the barbed wire fence. It was crazy to keep letting my mind run wild like this. No one was coming in the door. I was totally safe. The American ambassador himself had guaranteed our security. After about two minutes I got out of bed and stepped to the door. It was locked. I tried pulling it and it felt secure. I drew the chain anyway, and got back into bed.

Now the window was latched. The door was locked and chained. Barbed wire surrounded our building.

Guards were on duty. I shut my eyes. The whole death threat thing was probably just a publicity stunt, anyway.

I lay there. Ten minutes passed. Twenty. An hour. More. I glanced at my watch near the bed. It was well past midnight. I had never felt more awake in my entire life.

CHAPTER NINETEEN

A week of basketball practice, Ping-Pong, pinball, and long hours of watching Italian TV dragged slowly by. My nights were almost entirely sleepless. Now and then I would nod off for an hour or so, only to jerk awake at the slightest noise. Our team rarely left the fenced compound, and when we did we were always surrounded by a police escort and had no contact with fans or city dwellers.

Day by slow day, from watching CNN and talking to the few visitors we received, my teammates and I began to understand a little more about our situation and why such extreme security precautions were being taken. Augustus's comments at the press conference, and the ensuing death threat called into the newspaper, had drawn tremendous publicity all over Europe and back home in the United States.

On the one hand the governments of America and Italy felt that to send the tournament favorites home would be to appear to be giving in to neo-Nazis. With terrorism on the rise all over the world, it was felt that knuckling under to such pressure would merely invite more threats.

On the other hand, as Mr. Sullivan had said, there was reason to believe that the threat might be for real. If anything did happen to any of us, the sponsors of the tournament and the U.S. government were worried that they would be blamed, sued, and their strong stance against terrorism would be turned into an embarrassing defeat. The solution they apparently came up with was to let us stay in Italy if we wanted and our parents agreed, but at the same time to overprotect us so that nothing at all could possibly go wrong.

Our third tournament game, against Cuba, had a very different tone than any I had ever been in before. Metal detectors were set up at all the entrances to the arena, and police were everywhere. Before the start of the game *polizia* with guns strolled about at the edges of the hardwood, peering up into the stands.

When we first ran out of our locker room, down the narrow tunnel, and emerged suddenly into the bright lights in front of thousands of people, I was surprised to find how vulnerable I felt. It was like being naked. Maybe it was my imagination, but I was conscious of how many eyes were focused on me and me alone. Eyes from all over the arena, from front rows and from behind me. Of course I was eager to get the game underway, but part of me wanted to get under the bench and just lie there.

Once the game started, my jitters definitely affected my concentration. A fan would move or something bright would catch my eye, and I couldn't stop myself from looking. I turned the ball over half a dozen times.

As for hitting much-needed baskets from the outside, forget it. I couldn't even sink six-footers. Twice I put up embarrassing airballs that floated high over the hoop like blimps.

Coach Griffin took me out in the third quarter, with the score tied at fifty. "Not your night, Snowman," he said. "They're just not falling for you." Normally I would have been angry at having been taken out of a close game, but that night I felt relieved. I sat at the end of the bench, hunched over low, secretly glad to be out of the bright lights.

Some of the other starters were clearly off their games, also. Jorge was missing jump hooks. Stinger's baseline moves weren't clicking. Jamal, who they put in to replace me at guard, promptly missed a couple of wide-open shots.

It wasn't the best I had ever seen Augustus play, either. They were double-teaming him so he had trouble getting open, and he seemed to be having only a slightly better than average shooting night. But his concentration was razor sharp, and when it became clear that our team was in danger of losing to an inferior opponent, he picked up the slack.

Basketball may be a team game, but to win close ones, a team needs a "go-to guy." Someone must step forward and take control. That night, we rode Augie's shoulders to victory. Each time Cuba threatened to take the lead and pull away, he made a key steal or pulled down an offensive rebound to keep us right in the thick of it. On our last three possessions he took the ball inside, and all the Cubans could do was foul him. He stepped to the line six times and, looking straight into the frenzied Cuban cheering section behind the backboard, swished all six foul shots.

Watching him clinch the game, it was hard for me to believe there was a death threat hanging over his head. He might have grown up in a world very different from my own. He might be political in a way I couldn't understand. He might not want to shake my hand or even consider having me for a friend. But I had to admire him for being plenty tough.

Our victory against Cuba brought me little personal relief. My insomnia and nerves continued to get worse. I almost never went outside the compound building, even to walk around on the lawn behind the barbed wire fence. I spent most of my time reading and watching TV.

I reread *The Autobiography of Malcolm X*. The end of the book, where he is assassinated, had an awful lot more impact on me this time around. I remembered the end of the ride I had taken through South Central Los Angeles, when the cop had stopped our van and frisked us while his partner had kept a loaded gun trained on us. It's amazing that something as precious as a human life can be snatched away with just the slightest movement of an index finger on a curved piece of metal.

I watched game shows, movies, the news, and just about all the tournament basketball games that were televised. Before the death threat, we had often gone to the arena to watch the other teams play. Now, we assembled in the lounge to check out our competitors, watching them as blips on a TV screen, like millions of other people across Europe and around the world.

The Spanish team was clearly the class of the rest of the field. They were fast and well coached, and they had a forward named Ali who was quickly emerging as Augustus's competition for tournament MVP honors. Ali was part Moroccan — he had brown skin, long legs and arms, and an incredible head of shoulder-length dark hair. Even listening to the games in Italian, we could tell that the commentators were speculating on a final-round championship matchup between Spain and the United States. Augustus against Ali. Superstar versus superstar.

I never tried to call Janey, and I didn't spend too much time thinking about her. I guess maybe I was angry. This death threat thing made the picture in the newspaper seem ridiculous. How dare she get angry at me for such a silly misunderstanding? She had never called me or written me after I sent the roses, so I figured I would work things out with her when this was all over and I got back to Granham.

I wrote my mom a couple of letters, but from what I heard about the Italian mail, I would probably be back home before she got them. I called her twice, at home. Both conversations quickly deteriorated into me reassuring her how safe we were and how good I felt. In reality, I was tired and scared, and I didn't like the feeling of lying to her. Twice she tried to bring up Janey, but both times I changed the subject.

Instead of brooding about Janey or worrying about my mother, as I stayed awake night after night, I found myself thinking about my father. This was very strange, because whole years had passed when I had hardly ever thought about him. I almost never visited his grave. I rarely talked about him to my sisters, or to Janey. Sometimes, it had seemed as if my father had never lived at all — as if it had always been just my mom, my two sisters, and me.

William Doyle was a big man, more than six feet three inches in height and at least two hundred pounds. As I lay in bed through seemingly endless hours between midnight and dawn, staring up at the ceiling, I found I could recall my father's face with great accuracy. It was almost like projecting it from my imagination onto a movie screen. He had a shaggy red beard, ruddy cheeks, and merry black eyes. When I was very young, those eyes were always full of laughter and playfulness. He loved to kid around, tell jokes, and laugh in big belly-shaking bursts.

When I reached the age of ten, things started to go downhill. I was too young to understand the dip in our family's fortunes, but looking backward from the great distance of a silent room somewhere in the suburbs of Rome, the decline was mirrored by a new seriousness in my father's eyes. Even at ten I noticed the merriment slowly vanish, replaced by concern, then wariness, later worry, and finally by outright fear.

Our semifinal tournament game was approaching. We started double practices in the small gym they had found for us near our compound building. I wasn't playing particularly well, and all the guys knew it. Shawn tried hard to nudge me back into my game. "Just find your rhythm, Snowman," he'd say. "Once you sink a couple, you'll be the sharpshooter of old."

"No one can play basketball without any sleep," Coach Griffin told me. He gave me several nonprescription pills and herbs to help me sleep, but they had no effect whatsoever. He offered to take me to a doctor, but I told him not to bother. What was the point? I wasn't sick. Twice he asked me if I wanted to go home. "No one will hold it against you. You'll be safe and able to sleep at night." Even though I desperately wanted to take him up on his offer, I heard myself refuse. I guess I felt as if going back to America at this stage would be giving in to fear.

Every night I latched the window, locked and chained the door, closed my eyes, and waited for oblivion to descend. And every night I eventually surrendered in frustration to tossing, turning, and haunting memories.

The autumn before he passed away, my father suffered shortness of breath and an irregular heartbeat. I remember raking leaves with him, and watching him stop twice and stand very still, his fingers clenched tightly around the handle of the rake. Then he smiled at me and said, "Don't worry. It's nothing," and went on raking.

Just before Christmas he went into the hospital for tests that led to an operation. When he returned to the store he seemed physically much smaller, as if his medical ordeal had shrunk him. His hands shook so that his silverware clanked on his plate when he ate, and he would take a little white pill every few hours.

Ill fortune followed ill health, like two vultures slowly circling closer and closer. I remember Dad counting up the day's receipts from the store with his shaking hands, and exchanging worried glances with my mother. He forced himself to be so cheerful and enthusiastic to customers that I think he actually ended up making many of them nervous.

At a certain point, early that spring, he just sort of gave up. Fear is a terrible thing once it takes hold. I saw it as an eleven-year-old boy, and I was feeling it now as a seventeen-year-old man. It gets in the bloodstream and spreads throughout the body, from muscle to nerve, from brain to spine. If you've never watched a parent suffer through long periods of depression and ill health, consider yourself very lucky.

My father began to spend whole days and nights sitting on a chair in front of our old TV, watching just about anything. He kept the sound turned way down, as if the flickering black-and-white images were enough for him. Often, his eyes weren't fixed anywhere near the screen. He would sit there pretending to watch and shaking his head very slightly every few minutes.

He never gave voice to his thoughts, but then he didn't have to — his manner and expressions said it all: "It's over. There's no way we'll be able to hold things together. Whatever we do, however we struggle, debts and bad luck will pull us under." His eyes became red and sunken. The skin of his face took on the paleness of paper from a book that hasn't been opened in a long time.

Twice he tried to take out life insurance policies. Both times he was examined, and both times the insurance carrier rejected him as too high a risk. Those two attempts to get insurance were the very last efforts he made to help and protect his family.

Death soon preoccupied him. Some days he wouldn't want to get out of bed. My mother and I tried to keep our store running, even though in those days we knew very little about the hardware business. School had just ended for the summer, and I spent as much time as I could helping her out. We began to learn the stock, and to forge relationships with loyal customers.

Night after night I listened to my parents talking in the next room. Mom told him to go back to the hospital for more tests. He asked what the point was? They had done what they could for him. A psychologist, then, she suggested. To help battle this depression. What was the point of doing anything? he wanted to know. Then there usually came the awful sounds of my father breaking down and starting to cry. As a child, I had dug my face into my pillow and tried to drown it out. It usually ended with him telling her he loved her. Mom would reply that she loved him back, but that she was worried for our family.

In early March, my father died. As I've already described, I rode with him in the ambulance, and heard him whisper his last word, "Love." Later, I waited in the County Hospital in Chisholm while Dr. Sutherland labored to save his life. I remember sitting in an uncomfortable chair, tight faced, with my hands twisting themselves into endless knots. When we found out that William Doyle had lost his last battle, I broke down and cried, but at the same time I remember feeling a grim sort of relief that made me feel very guilty. At least it was over. At least fear no longer had a stranglehold over our home.

Now, in Rome, I couldn't go to sleep but I also couldn't go back to America. Sleepless nights merged into tired days. I kept more and more to myself. It was a strange and very depressing existence. Several times each day I was tempted to go to Coach Griffin and ask him to send me home, but I never did.

Deep down, I knew I had to stay and slug it out with my own fear of death, toe to toe, in the Eternal City.

CHAPTER TWENTY

If you don't know what it feels like to be hooted at by thousands of people in a foreign language, count yourself fortunate. In our semifinal tournament game we played the Italians. Nearly thirty thousand fans walked through the metal detectors to root for the home team. Every time an Italian player did anything right, thunderous applause shook the arena.

The only applause for us came when we missed shots. I quickly became the most popular American player on the floor. My shooting was so erratic that the Italian fans urged me to put the ball up whenever I had the chance. My shots bounced off the rim, clunked off the backboard, and airballed into the first few rows of seats. They did everything shots can do except fall through the hoop. Coach Griffin mercifully took me out in the middle of the second period.

The rest of our team wasn't quite as bad as I was, but they were also way off. The Italians responded to the cheers by fighting like tigers, and they led for much of the game. They might have pulled off a big upset against us if it wasn't for Augustus. Just as he had in the game against Cuba, in the crucial fourth period against

Italy, Augustus picked our team up on his back and carried us through to victory.

He staked his claim to the tournament MVP award with driving, slashing moves to the basket and jump-shots that swished the net from fifteen and twenty feet out. The Italian fans seemed to take his challenge personally, and for most of the game they jeered his every misstep. But Augustus played so flawlessly that they didn't have much to hoot about.

Augustus ended up with a triple-double: thirty-nine points, fifteen rebounds, and twelve assists. In the last two or three minutes, when it became clear that we were going to win, the Italian crowd showed good sportsmanship by cheering Augustus's last couple of sensational shots and brilliant feeds.

A few weeks ago, a game this close and a crowd this big and enthusiastic would have thrilled me — now it only spooked me. Dozens of *polizia* and *carabinieri* in uniform walked around with guns, looking upward through the rows for a face they knew or the flash of a gun being drawn. I found myself looking around with them, constantly scanning the crowd for anything out of the ordinary. I know it sounds crazy, but it wouldn't have surprised me at any point in the game if shots had suddenly rung out and everyone had fled for cover.

We celebrated our victory with a big lunch of gnoc-chi back in our compound building. Gnocchi are little dumplings, made from potatoes or flour. They have a terrific consistency — they're just a bit chewy and they soak up the sauce they're served in. In this case, the cook prepared big platters of both potato and wheat-flour gnocchi and served them with two very different sauces — a zesty red sauce filled with meat and a white one made with cream. The basketball game had made us pretty hungry, and after about half an hour of steady eating, every single gnocchi dumpling was successfully devoured. Shawn finished the last dozen or so himself, and announced that for the first time on this entire trip he had eaten his fill.

After the feast our whole team gathered in the lounge to watch the Spaniards play the Croatian team. It was a close and very physical game. In addition to Ali, their star, the Spanish team was powered by two superb guards, Vasquez and Castillo, who could both pop from the outside. The Croatians reminded me of the Germans — they were big, tough, and physical — but the Spaniards outran and outshot them. I could sense the excitement of my teammates in the lounge — it would be an interesting final game.

That evening Coach Griffin insisted on bringing a doctor to our compound to examine me. He spoke English and asked me a lot of questions about my insomnia and my eating habits. "He's perfectly healthy," he told Coach Griffin after the examination. "It's just a very bad case of nerves."

"Isn't it dangerous not to be able to sleep?" Coach Griffin wanted to know.

"If he continued this way for a long period, yes. But for a person this young and strong, for just a few weeks, it will not hurt him. I will give him some pills that may help him sleep."

I took the pills faithfully, but they didn't help all that much. If I was lucky, I would nod off for two or three hours.

"Man, maybe you should think about going home," Stinger suggested in the middle of the week. "I mean, if you can't sleep, you can't play."

Shawn nodded and gave me a friendly pat on my back. "You're thinking too much, Snowman. The secret to sleeping is not to think about it."

"Yeah, but if I think about not thinking, that starts me off thinking."

Shawn shook his head. "Snowman, maybe you really should go home. Love to have you help us whup Spain, but you gotta think about your health."

Augustus came up to me after our Wednesday morning practice and asked me why I was staying. "You're not helping us win and you look like death warmed over."

"It's just one more week. I'm gonna hang."

Augustus seemed to take this on some kind of personal level. "You don't have to hang — you don't owe anybody anything," he said. "Man, your eyes are sinking back into your head. Fly back to Minnesota and get a good rest."

I figure that a guy who didn't particularly want my friendship had no right to tell me I looked like death warmed over. "You take care of yourself. I'll watch out for myself," I told him.

On Thursday, two days before our big final game against Spain, the mayor of Rome came through on his promise to give us a private tour of the Colosseum. Coach Griffin told us about it at breakfast. "We're going to go in the late afternoon, just after they shut the gates to the general public," he said. "The embassy is supplying a guide. This'll be a great chance for you guys to do a little bit of sightseeing and take a break from thinking about B-ball."

At five o'clock we piled into a bus, and a police escort took us through heavy traffic to the Colosseum. The bus rolled up a driveway, right to the front gate. A dozen or so armed policemen were waiting there. They surrounded us and marched us through the gates, inside the spectacular old ruin.

The guide from the American embassy turned out to be a short woman in her mid-thirties with a serious face and a very loud voice. I'm not sure anyone at the embassy had told her that this was supposed to be a fun outing for us. From the first moment she greeted us and gave us her credentials, she was all business.

"The Colosseum was the largest and most famous of all the Roman amphitheaters," she began. "It was begun by the emperor Vespasian, dedicated to his son Titus, and completed by his younger son, Domitian. The exterior," her right arm swept around, "is a three-storied arcade surmounted by a fourth story with windowlike apertures. You can all feel how hot it gets even in the late afternoon. In antiquity, masts projected upward from the fourth story and supported enormous awnings that shaded spectators from the sun."

She led us forward so that we could peer down at where the ancient combats had taken place. A high wall ran completely around a big pit area. "Gladiators fought to the death here with swords. Sometimes a consistent winner and crowd favorite would be granted his freedom. But that was very rare. Gladiators were slaves, and usually the only escape for them was death."

She pointed to the high wall that ran completely around the arena. "That wall was necessary to keep wild beasts from escaping, and missiles and spears from endangering spectators. There, you see the *podium,* or platform, where the emperor had his box seat. Often, he would bring noble guests from around the world to sit with him. If he went like this," and she showed us a quick thumbs-down gesture, "death followed immediately."

She led us a little further toward the center of the oval and pointed out different subterranean halls and chambers. "We think those very large chambers may have been for water storage."

"Water for what?" Shawn asked.

"The floor of the Colosseum could be flooded into a little lake where naval battles were fought. Teams of slaves would be put in boats and forced to row out against each other, fighting to the death or drowning if their boats were overturned. And those pens over there were for animals."

"What kind of animals?" Jamal wanted to know.

"All kinds," she told him. "Often five thousand wild animals died here in a single day. Hunters spread through the far-flung Roman provinces, capturing lions, tigers, panthers, rhinoceroses, bears, and elephants. The demand was so great that entire species were wiped out — for example, the lion in Mesopotamia, and the elephant in North Africa. Animals from different corners of the world, that would never meet each other in nature, were matched for the first time in this arena. The crowds loved strange pairings, with both animals and humans. Dwarves were matched against women. Negroes — a real novelty — were matched against each other for enormous wagers."

"The Romans really liked to bet on fights to the death?" Jorge asked. "What sickos."

"It had a political use also," our guide told us. "The spectacles in the Colosseum were a way of controlling the masses. When the people were poor and lacked jobs or proper food, emperors would make sure there were spectacular games for them to watch. Fantastic spectacles would take their minds off their troubles."

She next launched into a list of measurements. I had heard enough, and edged away. Soon I was out of earshot.

Steep steps led up one level. I picked my way carefully — if I slipped, it would be a long and painful tumble. When I reached the *podium,* or platform level, I was surprised to see Augustus standing by himself, looking down into the center of the vast ruined arena. I guess he had slipped away from the lecture a few seconds before me. He was staring fixedly down as if he saw something in the ruins that fascinated and disturbed him.

We hadn't talked since the middle of the week, when I had told him to take care of himself and I would take care of myself. I don't think we had had a single real conversation since our ride together through the dark streets of South Central.

My footsteps padded off the old stone that had been worn smooth by centuries of curious sightseers. I walked by Augustus without saying a word, and about fifteen yards further on I came upon the jutting projection our guide had pointed out to us as the possible site of the emperor's box seat. I stepped out onto it. The wind blew my hair. It gave me a very strange feeling standing there.

Roman history isn't my strong point, but I had some sense of how Rome had dominated the ancient world. Caesars had stood in this very spot — the most powerful rulers on the planet.

I stepped farther out, to the very edge of the emperor's platform.

For the first time in weeks I was able to forget the whole death threat thing for a few moments. Two thousand years melted away beneath the sinking summer sun. I imagined myself in a flowing white robe, looking around at fifty thousand screaming subjects while gladiators waited for me to give the sign of life or death. I raised my arms, as if silencing the vast horde, and held out my right hand. And that was when Augustus walked up behind me and said, "Life or death, Snowman?"

I turned, a little embarrassed, and slowly lowered my right arm. "A place this full of history really makes you think," I mumbled.

He nodded, and his eyes flashed around the ruins of the ancient Colosseum, from fourth-floor attic to dusty pit. "You heard what the tour guide said about how the great spectacles here were used to take poor people's minds off not having money or jobs?" I nodded. "Well, I'm probably going to spend the best years of my life playing basketball in arenas kind of like this."

Augustus's ability to find the political side to just about anything never ceased to amaze me. The afternoon sun dipped beneath the highest of the arcades. "Basketball's a game," I said in a low voice. "It's not as if somebody's going to be forcing you to fight to the death. And if you make it as a pro, you'll earn millions of dollars."

"If it's just a game, how come we had to go into hiding and there are armed guards all around this arena?" I didn't even bother trying to answer. We stood in silence. The sun had completely disappeared, and a dark purple light spread itself over the old stones. Augustus surprised me by saying, "I've been worried about you lately, Snowman."

"I told you to take care of yourself and I'd worry about myself."

"You must've dropped fifteen pounds."

"Twelve."

He stepped forward on the emperor's platform so that he stood next to me. "It's a strange thing," he whispered. "My name comes from the greatest Roman emperor of them all. The emperor Augustus."

"Then maybe you should feel at home up here."

"To me this is an evil place. Even after two thousand years I can smell the fear and death."

"We always had very different takes on things. To me it seems kind of . . . thrilling. Like I can still hear the roar of the crowds."

We stood side by side. There was a long silence.

"So what've you been thinking about all these nights when you can't sleep?" Augustus finally asked.

I didn't answer for a long time. Finally I told him, "My father."

"Back in L.A., at the cemetery, you said you were with him when he was dying."

"And you said we had nothing in common and our fathers' deaths had nothing in common and then you walked away from me," I reminded him.

"What'd your old man die of?"

"Nothing as dramatic as yours. Just a bad heart."

"I guess that's tough, too."

"It wasn't much fun." I hesitated — and then for some reason I continued talking about something that I had never really talked to anyone about before. "The fear was the worst part of it."

"What fear?"

"The fear of death. It took everything away from him."

Augustus gave me a strange look.

"See, unlike your dad, mine knew he had it coming. My mother says he was peering into the abyss."

The guide and Coach Griffin had spotted us, and they were waving and shouting for us to rejoin the group. "Go back to Minnesota, Snowman," Augustus whispered. "Your father's been dead a long time. Whatever fear there was is long over. You can't help us win. We don't need you. So go home and at least help yourself."

Our eyes locked for a moment. "Your father's been dead a long time, too," I reminded him in a whisper. "But you won't shake my hand or call me friend." Then I turned and headed down the steps to rejoin our team.

CHAPTER TWENTY-ONE

On a map of Europe, Spain and Italy look pretty far apart, separated by enormous mountain chains of Pyrenees and Alps. But I guess with modern plane travel, express trains, and air-conditioned tour buses, the trip from Madrid to Rome is a fairly easy one. It seemed like half of Spain had made the long journey to shout *"Olé"* and cheer on their seventeen-and-under team in the tournament's final game.

We got to the arena early, warmed up in front of mostly empty seats, and then retreated to our locker room for a final team meeting. Our coaches closed the room off to the press, so it was just the team. "Guys, we've come a long way from our first meeting in the Wooden Center in Los Angeles," Coach McNeil told us. "A lot of practices, a lot of strange experiences, and a lot of tough games. I don't need to tell you what kind of dangers we've faced, or how proud I am that you all decided to stay in Italy and stick with it. Now, here we are — one more to win, and then we can go home."

Coach Griffin was even more to the point. "Some things that you do for only two hours stay with you your whole lives," he told us. "I promise you, this game will. Make sure that when the final buzzer sounds, you've given everything you had to give."

We joined hands. Jorge, who came from a religious background, said a prayer. There was a lot of energy and emotion in the circle of hands. And then we broke and headed out for our last four periods of basketball together.

I've got to give our coaches credit for loyalty — despite my condition and my previous two lousy games, they stuck with me as one of the starters. The few hundred or so Americans in the stands cheered as the Teen Dream Team was introduced. When I ran out onto the hardwood, I felt a lot of pride and also a sharp stab of fear. I knew this game was being televised live all over America. Mom, my sisters, and Janey were probably watching. If the neo-Nazi terrorists intended to make good on their death threat, this game would be their last chance.

Augustus got more cheers than the rest of us, and far, far more jeers, too. Boos, applause, and whistles cascaded down from the different stadium levels as he ran out to join the rest of us. Fans waved flags, threw confetti, and made obscene hand gestures. Augustus ignored it all. He slapped five with each one of us and then stood tall, letting the noise wash over him.

The Spaniards were introduced after us. Castillo and Vasquez, their two star guards, received lots of applause. When Ali, their handsome and super-talented forward and team captain was introduced, the Spanish fans in the arena went nuts. He seemed to be a special favorite of the female fans. I had never realized how beautiful Spanish girls can be. All around the arena I saw remarkable raven-haired beauties, with flashing eyes and flowers in their hair, rise to cheer Ali. He saluted them with a sweeping gesture of his right hand as he ran out to join his team, and I got my first clear look at him in person.

Ali was probably about six feet seven inches, with light brown skin and slightly darker eyes. Whenever he took a step, his long black hair tossed off his shoulders. By the standards of American athletes he wasn't particularly muscular, but just watching him jog out to take his place with his teammates, I could tell that he was something special. He moved with the kind of grace that God reserves for a handful of athletes in every generation. Augustus had it. Ali had it, too.

They played "The Star-Spangled Banner" and we stood at rigid attention. When they got to "The bombs bursting in air" I half expected the whole arena to go up in a blinding flash, but nothing happened. Then they played the Spanish national anthem.

Finally we were ready for basketball. We gathered around the circle, the ref threw the ball up, and Shawn tapped it back to Jorge. The seventeen-and-under world championship final game was on!

I hit my first outside shot, with Vasquez right in my face, and my teammates let me know how much they appreciated a little outside scoring. "That's it, Jimmy D!" Shawn shouted as we raced back upcourt.

"There's the Snowman of old!" Stinger said. "Ice it!"

Augustus nodded to me. "Way to shoot."

As I ran back to guard Vasquez on defense, I couldn't stop myself from thinking about Janey and my family and how strange it was that they were watching me live, half a world away. I bet there were some loud cheers in Granham when my first shot went in. The Sutherlands were no doubt watching on their wide-screen Sony color TV. In my mind's eye I could see my mother and two sisters sitting close to our nineteen-inch Zenith. I bet even the two little monsters were excited.

At the two-minute mark I took my second shot, from three-point range, and swished it to give us a lead. Despite all my tiredness, I was running well and seeing the basket well, and I thought maybe I might have a solid game.

Unfortunately, about a minute later, there was a disturbance in the fourth row. I heard shouting and saw police streaming over. I froze up on the court — my legs stopped moving and my arms went stiff, and all I could do was search the stands with my eyes for a gunman. It turned out that two spectators had begun pushing and shoving over a disputed seat, and order was quickly restored. But the disturbance spooked me. The game heated up after that, but I steadily cooled down.

Ali and Augustus put on quite a show, trading moves to the hoop, no-look passes to open teammates, and lightning-fast defensive steals. Five or six times Augustus kicked out passes to me, but each time as I released my shot I knew that I had missed. When Vasquez stole the ball from me at midcourt with five minutes to go in the first quarter, Coach Griffin took me out. "You gave us some good minutes," he said, trying to put things in the best possible light. "Scored some key baskets. Now, take a breather." But we both knew I was out of the game for good.

I sat there through the whole second quarter with a white towel draped over my neck, watching as Spain steadily pulled away. Jamal, my replacement, helped out with the ball handling, but he didn't have my range or touch and rarely shot. At the half, we were trailing by six.

We left the floor for the locker room. There were the usual speeches by coaches and players. Diagrams were drawn. New defensive strategies were discussed. Fists were thumped into palms. But none of it really mattered. We were going to lose to Spain, and everyone in our locker room knew it deep down in their hearts. Our coaches would never have admitted it, but they knew it. All of our players knew it. I knew it. Probably the only guy who didn't know it was Augustus, and that was because he was just plain too stubborn to admit the truth to himself.

Spain was as quick as we were. They were as well coached. Their guards could shoot better than ours, and Ali was every bit a match for Augustus. Plus, they were a hot team playing with confidence in front of enthusiastic fans, and we were a tired and scared team playing far from home under a death threat.

When we emerged from the locker room, a small group of our fans chanted "Teen Dream Team, Teen

Dream Team." A little girl with long blond hair woven into two braids and with braces on her teeth slowly waved a small American flag back and forth. When you see an American flag at such a moment, so far from home, it kind of makes you catch your breath.

I sat alone on the bench during the third quarter with the white towel pulled up over my neck and the back of my head, watching the game and occasionally glancing warily around at the fans. There were no further disturbances in the arena. Policemen with guns stood on either side of our bench, scanning the crowd at all times. Meanwhile, the Spanish team's lead kept growing. From six it jumped to eight. Then ten. Next time I looked it was fourteen.

Good teams make a last run before being whipped, and when the gap reached fourteen, the Teen Dream Team staged a desperate comeback bid. Shawn began ripping down offensive rebounds and putting them right back up. Augustus went on a tear. Together, they closed it to six points. Augustus made a sensational steal, beat all five of their guys on a breakaway, flew through the air from the foul line, and dunked the ball to cut their lead to four.

"Teen Dream Team. USA!" The few hundred Americans in the crowd made themselves heard. Coach Griffin and Coach McNeil both stood up, waved, cheered, and shouted advice. For just a moment it looked as if we might make it a close game after all.

Then big Shawn went down. I saw him leave his feet

to contest a rebound and land clumsily, planting his weight on the side of his foot. His usually happy baby's face twisted in a grimace of pain as he toppled slowly and majestically, like an old oak. Our two assistant coaches helped him limp off the floor. I had seen enough basketball injuries to know it was a bad sprain, and that he wasn't coming back.

With Shawn gone, our comeback disintegrated. The Spaniards' lead was soon back up in double figures. We had given our all and fallen short. The only person in the whole stadium who refused to acknowledge the obvious was Augustus. Double- and triple-teamed, he kept forcing his way to the basket. Twice I saw him go up with two Spanish defenders clinging to him, and still sink his shots. I took the towel from my neck and twisted it around and around in my hands. Near the end of the third period, I felt myself break out in a cold sweat.

Their lead reached sixteen just before the end of the third quarter. Augustus's eyes were blazing and when our other players gave up steals or missed shots badly, he shouted at them. I wasn't feeling very good at all. My palms were sticky with sweat. My body was trembling. On our last possession of the quarter, Augustus took the ball inside against three Spaniards and found some way to score. So we ended the quarter fourteen points behind.

During our coaches' instructions to us at the quarter break, I felt faint. I couldn't stop my body from trembling. When we broke our huddle, I walked over to

Coach McNeil and told him, "I don't feel so good. I think maybe I'm going to be sick."

He took one look at me and told our assistant coach to get me back to the locker room. The assistant coach didn't seem too happy about leaving the game, but he had no choice. We headed through the passageway, beneath the bleachers, and were soon back in our locker room. "Try some cold water on your face," our assistant coach said.

I splashed myself with freezing water, but it only made me feel worse.

"Do you want me to get a doctor?" he asked.

"No."

"Boy, Augustus is sure fighting hard," he said. "I've never seen anything like it. He's one tough guy."

I nodded, and then ran for a toilet stall and threw up. My body shook uncontrollably, so that I had to hold the edges of the toilet to brace myself. Our assistant coach looked nervous. "I really should get a doctor," he said. "You wait here."

He ran out and I was alone in the locker room. I stood up, walked to a sink, and rinsed out my mouth. I looked awful. I closed my eyes. A distant roar sounded from the fans in the arena. No doubt Ali had made another slashing move to the basket, or Vasquez or Castillo had sunk a long jumper.

I opened my eyes and looked at myself in the mirror. Ten or maybe fifteen seconds passed. I saw myself very clearly in that reflected image in the locker room beneath the stadium in Rome. James Giacomo Doyle at seventeen. Nothing special in any other way but basketball. B student. Can't dance. Can't sing. Not bad-looking but no Brad Pitt. Only one talent. A single God-given ability.

I had stopped shaking. Stopped sweating. Throwing up must have helped, somehow. My eyes, reflected in the streaked glass, were only eight inches away. They say that when a person is about to die, his life flashes before his eyes. I wasn't in any danger, but for a minute or so, striking images from my past and present jumped up before me in a stream of surprisingly distinct memories.

My father falling over in the hardware store, dragging his right hand along the counter. A siren and a blinking red light over a wet road. The day we buried him and my mother let out a single sob as the first shovelful of stony Minnesota earth landed on his coffin. My mom in her rocker, a towel across her eyes. Janey. She had felt so light in my arms on our last day together, on the banks of the stream that fed Otter Lake.

Another roar came from the arena.

I left the mirror and began to walk. The sweating and the trembling had completely stopped. I felt strange. Not good and not bad, but oddly numb. Almost outside of my own body. A short corridor. A heavy door. Step by step. The lights and sounds of the arena opened up in front of me. Soon I was halfway down the aisle that led past the front rows of seats to the hardwood.

The game clock said that there were nine minutes left. We were fifteen points behind. As I watched, Augustus tried to fight his way to the hoop against a double team. A third Spaniard came over so that he was triple-teamed. The three Spaniards managed to strip the ball from him. The crowd roared.

I found myself walking again, toward our bench. Coach McNeil was sitting with his arms crossed rigidly against his chest. Coach Griffin was standing up, hands on his hips, shaking his head slowly back and forth as if denying something. I squeezed my way between them, and tapped Coach McNeil on the shoulder. He glanced at me. "You okay?"

I nodded. "Put me in."

"What?"

"No one can score against a triple team. Put me in."

Coach Griffin glanced over at me. "Sit down, Snowman."

"Yeah, sit down," Coach McNeil said. "This isn't your night, tonight."

My eyes met Coach Griffin's eyes. "You came all the way to Minnesota to get me for just this moment. Give me the chance to do what you brought me here to do."

"GO SIT DOWN," Coach McNeil said much more loudly.

I looked into Coach Griffin's eyes. His mustache twitched. Then I walked over to the end of the bench, but I didn't sit. I just stood there, hands at my side, looking out over the court.

Augustus fed a terrific pass to Jamal, who put up a jumpshot. It rimmed out. The Spaniards lead was eighteen. Eight minutes and thirty seconds left.

I saw Coach Griffin whisper something to Coach McNeil. Coach McNeil shook his head. More whispering. Finally Coach Griffin gestured for me to come. "You're in at the next whistle for Jamal, Snowman," he said. He put a hand on my shoulder. "I remember the first time we saw you play, back in that old gym in your little town. You were pretty hot stuff that night."

I glanced back at him, and felt myself almost smile. Seeing it, he almost smiled back. Then he pushed me toward the scorer's table.

I knelt in front of the table, waiting for a stoppage of play. The American play-by-play announcer was in the second row, and I heard him say, "It looks like number sixteen, Jimmy Doyle, is going in. That's Jimmy Doyle from Granham, Minnesota, a shooting guard . . ."

A whistle sounded. I ran in. Jamal ran off. Eight minutes and seven seconds left.

Augustus brought the ball up for us, and took it into the right corner. The Spanish defender bodied up against him. He spun inside and tried to drive the baseline, but Ali was waiting there. A third Spanish player ran over. Augustus leaned forward, using all of his strength to break through the wall of defenders for just a second. He spotted me, and suddenly the basketball was in my hands.

Without even thinking, I set my feet, found the hoop, and shot from two steps behind the three-point line. Look. Release. Arc. It felt short as it left my fingers, but the ball kissed the front of the hoop, rolled around twice, and dropped. We were losing by fifteen.

Vasquez was a slick ball handler. I stayed in front of him, backing up, backing up, watching his eyes. His center of gravity started to shift and I anticipated his move and dove in, slapping the ball. It bounced through his legs and Augustus was there to scoop it up. I recovered quickly and the two of us flew downcourt, against three Spanish defenders. Augie passed it to me. I took it left, pulled up at the foul line, pumped, and then threw a lob to Augustus, who slipped behind his man and jammed it home with one hand.

Thirteen points.

Our next time down, I stayed far outside, sliding around the perimeter. At the last moment Augustus flipped the ball to me. Vasquez came sprinting out, hands waving in the air. I elevated. When I reached the peak of my jump and saw the hoop, I couldn't believe it. The orange rim was ten feet wide. It was a Grand Canyon! No one could miss a rim that big. I let the ball go. Swish.

I don't know if you've ever been in a zone. There's nothing else like it in sports. There's probably nothing else like it in life. Who knows why you slip into one? Or why you suddenly fall out of it? But when and if you ever do find the magical doorway, watch out, because for a few minutes you'll be capable of just about anything.

The Spaniards fought hard to hold their lead. They put bodies on me and they doubled up on Augustus, and they continued to play aggressive offense. But they were in trouble. Because two Teen Dream Team members were in a zone — two of us in the same weird magical zone — and neither one of us could miss.

Their lead was ten. Augustus sank a fadeaway jumper with four hands in his face. He's in a zone. I'm in a zone. Zone, zone, zone! Slam it home!

I faked my outside jumpshot. Two of their guys sailed up in the air to block it. I dribbled in, saw Ali standing beneath the basket, switched hands as I flew through the air, and banked the ball in off the glass. Zone, zone, zone. We were in a serious, perilous, querulous zone.

Their lead was eight. The crowd had gotten mighty quiet.

The Spanish coach called time-out. Our coaches talked. Words flew by me. Everything was poetry. Augustus and I traded looks. Odd to be in a zone with someone else. Same team. Same game. Zone, zone, zone.

Back on the floor. Ali had the ball. Augustus was marking him. MVP on MVP. Move on move. Fakes. More fakes. I left my man and darted in behind him. Ali sensed my approach at the last second and tried to dribble away, but Augustus alertly reached in and swatted the ball.

Jorge came up with it. He passed it to me on the left side. Vasquez and Castillo were both running with me. I got only a split-second glance at Augustus and Ali sprinting down the center of the court. Augie had a half-step lead. I turned away from the basket as if I was going to take the ball back outside, and then I pivoted and threw a no-look pass toward the hoop. Ali reached for it but it was just beyond his fingertips. Augustus some-how hauled it in, launched himself from an awkward angle, turned halfway around in the air, and dunked the ball with both hands.

The lead was six. Screens and picks.

The lead was four. Slam the door.

Time-outs interrupted the flow of the game but they didn't matter. The screaming of the fans didn't matter. Hard fouls didn't matter. Augie and I were deep into a serious zone. It was an untouchable, unreachable place.

The lead was two. Less than a minute left. Ali hit a three-pointer — I had to give the guy credit, he was playing two Teen Dream Teamers in a zone and still fighting back.

Five points. Less than a minute.

I took the ball up. Saw Augie triple-teamed. Jorge made a cut under the basket. I threw him a blur of a pass. He went up strong and jammed it home, drawing a foul. Three-point play. Their lead was two.

Fifty seconds left. Forty-five. There is no shot clock in seventeen-and-under basketball. The Spaniards could pass the ball back and forth and just run out the last half minute. They were good athletes, in superb condition, and they worked the ball skillfully around. The thing to do was to foul them, but each time we tried they'd throw a long pass to an open man.

Twenty-five seconds left. Twenty. Fifteen. Ten. Augustus left his man and darted into a passing lane.

Somehow, he came up with a clean steal. Immediately we all signaled for a time-out. Seven seconds.

We gathered around our coaches on the bench. Words and plans registered from far away. Shawn was coming back in for the final play, bad ankle and all. He would set up at the top of the key. Jorge would inbound the ball and look for Augustus or me. If either of us got it, we were to try to penetrate. If all the lanes were closed, we were to pass it to Shawn, who would find the open man. "We don't need a three-pointer," Coach Griffin said. "Just a regular basket ties it. Work for a high percentage shot. Get inside!"

Then we were running back on for the final seven seconds. The crowd was on its feet. The Spanish team had the lead, and in a few heartbeats they could have the game and the tournament, too.

I had never felt so alive. The action seemed to slow way, way down. I had been in zones before, but never of this depth and clarity. Seven seconds were an eternity. Shawn limped to the top of the key. The ref handed Jorge the ball.

Seven seconds. I broke one way and Augustus broke another way and Jorge threw it to Augie. Six seconds. Five. Augustus dribbled upcourt. Ali and Castillo were all over him. Somehow he got off a pass to Shawn at the top of the key. Four seconds. Shawn held the ball high up above his head, searching for a pass.

I drifted far out on the left side. Vasquez was right on me. Shawn looked for the pass inside to Jorge. Covered.

He looked back at Augustus. Double covered. He looked for any pass. Panic showed on his face. Three seconds. Two. He threw me an awkward floater. Vasquez probably could have stolen it but he didn't want to foul, so he let me catch it. One second. I turned toward the hoop, fell back into an awkward fadeaway, and threw up a prayer from at least forty feet out.

My clumsy fadeaway took me backward, down onto my rear end. Vasquez landed on top of me. The buzzer sounded and the crowd roared. I tried to spot the hoop through the tangle of arms and legs, to see what had happened to my shot. I finally located the white netting, just as an orange sphere of basketball dropped almost straight down, swishing the cords.

Pandemonium broke out. I turned my head toward our bench and saw Coach Griffin jump at least two feet in the air, his hands folded into fists, punching toward the ceiling with his right hand. Augie and Shawn were running toward me.

I got back to my feet and took a step toward them, my arms raised in victory, and just at that moment, a serious-looking little man in a dark suit broke through the police lines and ran out onto the floor. He was looking past me, to Augustus. His right hand disappeared for a split second and then reappeared with a small gun.

I was seeing the world in an unusual, crystal-clear way that you may not know or understand if you haven't played sports at a top level. Everything registered. A young Italian policeman dove at the little man from behind, just as he raised the gun. I tried to run out of the way. The policeman hit the little man's shooting arm. There was a red flash and a single popping sound, and then the policeman tackled the little terrorist.

My first thought was that I was still alive. He must have missed.

Then I felt myself begin to fall over on my right side, and I realized that something was very wrong.

CHAPTER TWENTY-TWO

I was descending through clouds, gently and slowly. Soft music played. Janey's hand was in mine, her breath on my cheek.

We had been sitting that way, close, without talking, for hours. Her hand was warm. Once, she turned my hand palm up, as if preparing to tell my fortune, but instead she just gave it a quick kiss. The clouds thinned out and bright blue ocean gleamed far beneath. And then Dr. Sutherland crossed the aisle and began to explain about the Semilunar Fibro-cartilages, and how they serve to deepen the surfaces of the head of the tibia. I kept hold of Janey's hand as he interspersed his descriptions with glowing accounts of Dr. Veederman's credentials as a microsurgeon.

Janey squeezed my hand. "Dad, maybe Jimmy doesn't feel like talking about this . . . ?"

"I like talking about it," I told her. And then, to her father, "It's funny, before this all happened, I always thought all doctors were pretty much the same."

"Not at all," Dr. Sutherland assured me. "Veederman's supposed to be the best in the entire country. The list of pro athletes who've been worked on by him is remarkable."

The plane landed and taxied in. All of the other passengers got off. I was loaded into my wheelchair and Janey pushed me out of the jet, through the passageway. A big press contingent was waiting for me at the gate. "He'll talk to you after the operation," Dr. Sutherland announced, but I wasn't surprised that he was ignored.

Microphones were pushed in my face. A photographer collided with my wheelchair, nearly upsetting it. Questions, both appropriate and inappropriate, were shouted at me. "Is it true that you've been invited to the White House next month?" "How did you pick this doctor in San Diego?" "What are the odds that you'll play basketball again?"

I smiled, waved, and kept my mouth tightly shut till Dr. Sutherland and Janey somehow got me past them. The last few days had been an education in politics and the press.

A noted specialist had been rushed in from Milan for the first operation. When I regained consciousness, he told me I was very lucky. If the bullet had been a fraction of a millimeter to either side, the damage to my knee would have been much more serious. As it was, he felt that with proper rehabilitation, there was a slight chance I might be able to play again someday. A second operation would be necessary, and maybe even a third. They asked me if I wanted to have the operations done in Rome.

I spent a few long and dark days lying in that Roman hospital room, turning everything over in my mind. I was cheered by visits from my Dream Teammates, who came in groups of two and three, escorted by security guards. Shawn brought me a bunch of newspapers, and there was my picture on half a dozen different front pages. Jorge and Stinger gave me the ball from the Spain game, signed by the players from both sides. It sat on a chair near my bed, a reminder of what I had done, and what I might not be able to do again. Augustus never came to visit. I guess I understood that. As he had made clear all along, we were teammates but not friends. After three days in that hospital room, I asked the Italian doctors to please send me home. I told them I had my own personal medical advisor in Granham, Minnesota, and that I would like to have the other operations done in America.

You can't imagine the fuss when I got back to Granham. It was like I was some kind of war hero. TV news crews practically camped on our doorstep. Politicians, local, state, and even national, called to wish me well and invite me to meet with them. A congressman came by unexpectedly the morning after I arrived to have his picture taken shaking my hand.

At first all the attention was a little thrilling. Then the inappropriate questions, the invasiveness of the reporters, some of whom took pictures through our windows, and the false sympathy of the politicians who showed up at our apartment to turn my injury into photo ops, started to get a bit much. When reporters who I had talked to at length wrote stories that made me sound angry, or even worse, pitiful, I stopped giving interviews.

I wasn't angry. In fact, I felt oddly at peace. I was sleeping ten hours a night, and waking up fresh and clear-headed. I couldn't even imagine not being able to play basketball for the rest of my life, so I didn't dwell on it. Instead, I enjoyed returning home to the town where I had grown up and the people who loved me.

It turned out that my mother and sisters had been watching the final game at the Sutherlands' house, and that when I was shot Janey had become hysterical. She was there to welcome me when my plane landed, and give me the sweetest kiss in the history of Minneapolis–St. Paul International Airport.

It took us about twenty seconds face to face to solve all our problems. She thanked me for the roses and said that she had been desperately trying to call me all during our last two weeks in Rome, but the American embassy wouldn't give out a phone number for us. I explained to her about the photograph that had caused all the trouble, and we agreed to just put the misunderstandings behind us.

I got pretty good treatment at home. Mom surprised me by serving up a rack of lamb for my first dinner stateside. "It's been a while since I cooked anything like this," she said. "Is it okay?"

"Let me put it this way," I told her. "For a meal like this, I'll get shot any day of the week."

One of the strangest things about my new celebrity was that our hardware store suddenly became busier than it had ever been. It seemed as if everyone in our town, from the mayor on down, stopped in once a day to say hello to my mother and buy something. In addition to Janey, who worked there part time, both of the little monsters were helping out during the day. To my surprise, they seemed to enjoy working and were both learning the stock at an incredible speed. I guess it really is easier to learn things when you're young.

My mom couldn't decide whether or not to fly west with me for the operation. Ever since my father had died, she had been uncomfortable in hospitals. Also, business at the store was roaring along, and if Mom came she would have to close up for half a week and find someone to watch my sisters. "You decide," she finally said. "I'll be happy to come if you want me there."

"Since Dr. Sutherland and Janey are coming, I'll be in good hands," I told her. "You should stay."

The flight west reminded me a bit of my flight to Los Angeles to the Teen Dream Team's training camp. We even had a little air turbulence. One difference was that this time I flew first class. The sponsors of the basketball tournament were picking up all my bills, and they seemed to be going out of their way to treat me well. Dr. Sutherland said they were worried that I might try to sue them for failing to protect me.

During the flight, two flight attendants came over to tell me they'd watched the tournament on TV and to wish me well. One of them even asked me for an autograph. It's strange to realize you've become something of a celebrity.

My first day in San Diego was spent taking X rays and other tests. Dr. Veederman was a friendly guy with big black eyes that seemed too large for his thin and angular face. "I hear you're the best," I said when I first met him.

"I watch a lot of basketball and you're pretty good yourself," he told me. "We'll see what we can do about getting you back in action. But . . ." he hesitated . . . "Jimmy, I must tell you, I'm not a miracle worker."

I nodded. "Just do what you can for me."

At ten the next morning I found myself in a private room of the hospital, about to be prepped for surgery. Janey was there, and Dr. Sutherland. I was kind of surprised when the door opened and Coach Griffin walked in. Augustus LeMay was right behind him. Both were wearing dark suits. Janey and Dr. Sutherland recognized them from our televised games, and introductions were quickly made all around.

"Just wanted to wish you good luck, Snowman," Coach Griffin said. "Since I persuaded you to come in the first place, I thought I should be here. And I brought something for you." He fished a little jewelry box out of his pocket and handed it to me.

I opened it. Resting on a tiny blanket of blue velvet was a silver ring, similar to an NBA championship ring. It had the date of our victory engraved inside, and said *Junior World Champions.* I took it out of the box and slipped it on my finger.

"Thanks. Thanks for coming," I told Coach Griffin.

"I'll see you after the surgery," he said.

"Good luck and just try to relax," Dr. Sutherland told me. "You're in the very best hands." Then he and Coach Griffin walked away.

Augustus had been conversing with Janey. Now that the three of us were alone in the room, he came over. True to form, he didn't hold out his hand for a shake, but he did give me a smile. "Hey, Snowman, you got a mighty fine girl here. I don't know what she's doing with a guy like you."

"I'm a woman, not a girl," Janey told him. "And I'm with him because he's the best three-point shooter in the world."

Augustus gave her a look that said, "You haven't seen me try to shoot from that range."

"What's with the suit?" I asked him. "You look like you're going to a funeral."

"It's my church suit."

"This isn't a church."

A nurse stuck her head in. "One minute," she said. She withdrew, and there was an awkward silence in the room. I decided to break it. "So what are you doing here?" I asked Augustus.

"What do you mean, what am I doing here?"

"I mean, we're not really friends, right? Did you just happen to be passing by on the highway?"

"Ease up, Snowman." He looked very uncomfortable. "I'm here 'cause I wanted to be here."

"I'm not trying to make things rough for you, but if I have to go in for a critical operation, I want to be surrounded by my friends."

Janey was confused. She kept looking from one of us to the other.

"I could never make you out, Snowman," Augustus said. He tried to smile and joke his way out of it. "All I know is for a honky from Minnesota, you played a hell of a basketball game. That last shot was something."

I nodded. "You're right, we played a great few minutes of basketball together. Thanks very much for coming by. It's a long drive from L.A. and I appreciate your taking the time. Now why don't you leave so I can be with my girlfriend?"

Augustus took a few steps toward the door. Then he turned. He looked almost angry. "Damn you, Snowman. You know why I'm here. You took my bullet."

"Is that it? Guilt? Well, don't worry, I was trying to get out of the way."

He walked back over to me, and stood just above my stretcher. "What do you want me to say?"

"I didn't even ask you to come here."

"But I came."

"Great. Thanks. Good-bye."

"STOP IT!" Janey shouted. And then in a lower voice she said, "Whatever's going on, just stop it. It's not the place for this . . ."

The nurse came back into the room. "It's time," she said.

Augustus and I looked at each other. Neither of us said a word.

"Can I wheel him down the hall?" Janey asked the nurse.

She looked a little surprised, but she nodded. "Sure. At least some of the way."

Janey expertly released the brake and then walked to the front of the gurney and began to pull it. "You've done this before," the nurse said.

"Both my parents are doctors," Janey told her.

Augustus trailed us down the corridor and then speeded up till he was walking alongside me, helping Janey propel the gurney forward. I felt his right hand fumble awkwardly for my own. "You stupid Minnesota honky hick geeky son of a bitch," he whispered. "I hope this operation's a success so that I can whup your butt all over a basketball court."

"Come on out to Minnesota," I told him, "and we'll go one-on-one in the snow."

Janey swung around to the other side and took my left hand. I spotted Dr. Veederman twenty yards ahead, donning a surgical mask. My heart beat a little bit faster, but there was no fear. I closed my eyes, lowered my head back onto the pillow, and let the stretcher carry me on down the long, smooth hospital hallway.